Paddy and Daryl
in the Elfic Realm

Monique Sivelle McCracken

PublishAmerica
Baltimore

First printing

ISBN: 1-4137-7780-5
PUBLISHED BY PUBLISHAMERICA, LLLP
www.publishamerica.com
Baltimore

Printed in the United States of America

Acknowledgment

To my husband who encouraged me in my new adventure as a writer and who opened the magic world of computers to my imagination. Then I typed "Once upon a time…" and Paddy was born.

Many thanks to my good friend Don Farrow who believed in me and to all my dreaming friends who loved my stories.

Monique and Paddy

Preface

Paddy, now is an elfic prince. He is the son of King Ariol and Queen Tara, his earthly mother. At eleven, Paddy had bravely freed his father from the evil claws of Wargo the Sorcerer with the power of the magic Flaming Sword.

The young prince, Patrick, has just turned his fifteenth elfic year, an important step for a young elf. From now on, like any of the other people of the realm, he would age very slowly. Paddy had left Earth Realm four elfic years ago, an extremely short time for his new realm. However, Daryl, his childhood friend, is now an old man according to earth time.

Chapter 1

Paddy walked in the park, deep in thought and kicking a stone. Under the shade of the trees he pondered the sad fact that soon his friend would reach the end of his mortal life. Absently, he watched the dogs, Tiger and Mitsou, frolicking around. They were still young. His mind wandered back to Daryl, his old buddy.

Paddy kicked the stone vigorously muttering, "I should do something! But, what?"

Tiger stopped playing with Mitsou and dashed to Paddy, halted in front of his master. The dog boldly barked wagging his tail.

Paddy laughed, hugged Tiger and skipping, shouted, "Of course, boy! I will return to the cliffs. I will!"

Quickly, Paddy left the playing dogs and talking to himself said, "I must talk immediately with Uncle Niko."

On his way to the palace, he met his cousin Stoy.

"Paddy, how about coming to the academy for some fencing practice?"

"Okay. Later. I need to talk to Niko first."

"Fine. See you there."

Paddy ran. Excitedly, he bolted into Niko's study, shouting, "Uncle Niko, Uncle Niko! I want to help my friend, Daryl. You remember him, don't you?"

"Of course, I do. The one always in trouble."

"Right!" Paddy laughed. "I wanted so much to be like him."

His uncle smiled and said, "It was not in your nature, Paddy."

"Maybe." The young elf stayed silent for a moment and said, "I want to bring him to the realm. I can do that. I know enough magic now, and my power is getting stronger."

"I know. Whatever you do will be all right. You are a good boy, Paddy."

"All right!" shouted Paddy. Lighthearted, the boy ran to the academy.

Early the next morning, Paddy left for the Earth Realm. There he sat on the edge of the cliff with his legs dangling in the air. He chuckled, remembering how scared he had been of everything. He looked up and smiled at the seagulls following the air currents, joyously wheeling and squawking. How he had wished he could fly…and now!

The morning went by. No sign of Daryl. Paddy's heart missed a beat. What if he was too late? What if Daryl was dead?

Then, in the afternoon around four o'clock, he heard a shuffling. Daryl had arrived. Paddy sighed with relief.

Grumpily, Daryl asked, "What are you doing here? This my place."

"Excuse me." Paddy got up.

Still grumpy, Daryl said, "I guess, old man, you may stay where you are."

"Thank you." Then Paddy realized that he, too, being on earth appeared old.

Daryl, from under his white brows, was looking at Paddy's green leather hat, beige pants, white satin tunic, and brown boots. Gruffly he asked, "Why are you dressed up like that, old man? Are you from the circus?"

"No, I am an elf."

"An elf! I haven't heard that one for a long time!" Daryl laughed.

"Yes, I am, and if you want, I will tell you splendid stories of my realm."

"I am too old for stories, friend, and you are too. I had a very dear chum in my youth, who was an elf, a real one! His name was Patrick. We called him Paddy. We had such good times together. We were young." With regret he sighed. "He was a prince in his realm. I certainly would have liked to live in such a magic place."

"Everything is possible, Daryl, if you dream hard enough"

"How do you know my name? Yes, when you are young, all dreams are real, I know," replied Daryl with clouds of longing in his eyes.

Paddy quietly cloaked himself and became invisible. He patiently waited and watched. After a while, Daryl realized he was alone. He sighed, and painfully leaning upon his heavy stick, he got up. Early spring in Ireland is cold. Daryl draped his brown coat tightly around his frail body, pulled his red toque over his ears, and walked back to the village.

Paddy, still invisible, walked beside him and silently chuckled. He could hear Daryl muttering, "The old man must be crazy, imagining himself as being an elf. I haven't seen any since Paddy, and that was a long time ago!" His heavy shoes shuffled the dirt as he continued talking to himself. "I've been there, couldn't return. Shouldn't have given the ring back to Paddy." Daryl made a sort of grunt and said, "I am glad my mind is still sound."

Every afternoon Daryl stopped at the pub to play cards. Of course, he didn't dare to tell the men about the encounter on the cliffs. Bitterly he mumbled, "They would think I've lost my marbles. Funny that I should put it that way. That's how Paddy would have said it."

The card games finally were over. Thank goodness, thought Paddy, still invisible, stretching his legs. While invisible, Paddy was reverting to his youth. He left with Daryl for home, but Daryl was waking so slowly that Paddy allowed himself a little sprint on the road.

The sweet smell of the apple trees in bloom brought Paddy back to his evening racing with his chum on their skateboards. Paddy silently chuckled.

They arrived at Daryl's rundown house. Daryl never had been good at helping his father around the farm. Dick, his beige-brown dog, came to greet him at the gate, barking joyously with a husky voice and wagging tail. Curiously, he sniffed the invisible Paddy, who gently scratched the dog's head.

"Hi, old friend. How was your day? Did you chase a coney?" Daryl patted Dick who jumped as much as his arthritic legs

9

permitted. "Let's go in, boy. We will have good hot soup with bread, cheese and an apple. How about that?"

Of course, Dick agreed with the idea. For a reason he couldn't explain, Daryl was happy. That night he slept like a baby, and Dick peacefully snored at the foot of the bed.

Chapter 2

Next morning Daryl woke feeling marvelously rested. The sun shone brightly in the room. Paddy couldn't say the same thing. He had slept on a bench downstairs. His fifteen-year-old body, used to a soft bed, didn't like it at all.

Paddy heard Daryl cheerfully saying to his dog, "My friend, after breakfast we are going for a nice walk in the forest."

Dick barked approvingly.

Daryl's heavy footsteps were coming down the stairs. A few minutes later, the smell of hot chocolate filled the kitchen. Breakfast over, Daryl took his walking stick, and they left. Paddy promptly pulled out some elfic biscuits from his pocket and drank the leftover chocolate before he dashed through the door.

Their walk took them to a copse of trees, which Daryl had taken to calling a forest. That morning it really did look like a forest with surprisingly soft moss underfoot. The shade was inviting. Daryl sighed and sat on a big stump, shaped like a high-backed chair He had never seen it before.

As he closed his eyes, the earth shook, and a loud voice asked, "What do you want?"

Chapter 3

Terrified, Daryl looked around. "Who's talking?" he asked, with a shaky voice.

"I am Woltar, genie of the forest."

"There is no genie in this forest. I know it. I have been coming here for nearly a century."

Still invisible, Paddy chuckled.

"Are you calling me a liar?" asked the Genie angrily.

"Yes! Don't take me for a fool. Show yourself. Stop hiding."

Dick whimpered.

"All right," replied the voice. The leaves twirled under a powerful wind, and a gigantic personage appeared dressed in baggy yellow pants. He was bald, except for a long, dark braid starting at the top of his head and almost reaching his feet. Around his neck a heavy gold chain hung with a large gold locket, which had a huge, green emerald in the center. "Now, I ask you again, what do you want? Why are you sitting in my chair?"

Daryl was so scared that no words came out of his mouth. Once again the voice thundered. Daryl, now terrified, sprang from the stump and Dick barked, his hair standing up on his spine.

"Speak, little man!"

Paddy, watching Daryl, almost burst into laughter.

"But, but," he spluttered. "Where do you come from?" he finally asked. "I have never seen you before. Are you from a circus visiting our town?"

"A circus," thundered the giant, outraged. "You have never been in my forest before, little man."

"But, but, I have been coming here since I was a child.'"

"Oh, no, you haven't," interrupted the genie.

"Listen! I am not crazy!" cried Daryl, getting angry. "I may be an old man, but I am not a fool."

"Who said you were an old man?" asked the genie.

"I did! And I am."

"Well, then, look at yourself."

"What do I have that is so remarkable that I have to look at myself?" replied Daryl, red and now really furious.

In his anger he glanced at his hands. They were the hands of a young man! Daryl, astonished, continued. "You asked me to look at myself. If you are a genie, give me a mirror."

A large mirror appeared in front of the old man. What he saw left him speechless. He was a young boy of fifteen, and Dick was a young dog. He was dressed in his old jeans with fringes at the bottom and holes at his knee. Dirty white sneakers covered his feet and turned backward was his greasy red baseball cap on his head. Over his arm was a cape. "How did this happen?"

"You are in the Elfic Realm," thundered the Genie.

"What? In the Elfic Realm? Impossible! How did I get here?"

"I don't know. Tell me what you want now."

"I want to see the old elf who came to visit me on earth."

"Why? He is right beside you! So your wish is granted earthly man." The genie disappeared in a twirl of leaves, the same way he had come. In his place stood an elf of about fifteen.

"Dirty fellow. He tricked me. I asked for the old elf, not for you," yelled Daryl, furious.

"Calm down, Daryl. I am the old fellow."

"What! How do you know my name?"

"I am Paddy, your friend. Don't you recognize me?"

"Honestly, nope! When you left, you were a very young lad, and so was I."

"I am not that old, only fifteen, man, and so are you!" Paddy laughed and slapped his friend on the shoulder. "I am mighty glad you are here, man! I really missed you. Life was kind of dull without you."

"Nothing was as much fun after you left," replied Daryl with a chuckle. "Tell me, man, how did I come here?"

"I brought you, and your house, to the edge of the Enchanted Forest when you were asleep."

His eyes rounded in surprise. Daryl looked at him. "What! How did you do that?"

"You remember my Uncle Niko, the wizard? Well, he discovered, that, like him, I too, am a wizard."

"Wow! Cool, man. A wizard!"

"Yes, he has helped me to develop my gift. Now, don't play any bad tricks on me, man, or I will change you into a toad." Both laughed heartily.

"I haven't laughed like that for a long time. I have to thank you for giving me back my youth. Wow! This is cool! Young again!"

"That part is not my doing. It's the Realm. Elves are young forever. If you decide to stay here you must become an elf, otherwise, being a mortal, you will grow old and soon die, like on earth."

"If I want? You bet, man! How do I do that?"

"Stay cool. Don't be so jumpy. It's not urgent. I will arrange the matter, later on with my father, the King, if it's still your desire."

"You bet it's my desire! I want to stay with you! See my dear old Dick, he is a bouncing puppy!"

While the two young men were talking and laughing about old times on earth, Paddy heard a shuffling. The young elf touched Daryl's sleeve and put his finger to his lips. Quickly, they hid behind a bush.

A giant white furry creature, walking upright, appeared. He had a horsey face, and his large gentle eyes were full of tears. Behind each pointed ear sprung short horns. Painfully dragging his flat feet on the grass, the giant's big hands rubbed his head, and he groaned softly.

"He doesn't look mean," said Daryl.

Chapter 4

The boys stepped out showing themselves. "No, it's Vald. He is a gentle creature. Hello, Vald. What are you up to?"

Vald jumped in terror and let out a whinny.

"Don't be afraid. It's I, Paddy. Why are you so scared?"

Vald looked around anxiously. "The Sorcerer Xary is after me."

"Why?"

"He wants my horns to make a powerful magic tool. When my horns are gone, I won't have any power of my own left." Big tears rolled down on his furry face.

"Who's Xary?" asked Daryl.

"A lesser sorcerer, a nasty one. Don't worry Vald, we won't let him do that to you."

Vald sighed. "Xary almost got me. He threw a spell so hard on my head, it still hurts."

"The evil one terrorizes our people. I asked my father, the King, to send me on a quest to destroy him. Would you like to come with us? Vald, meet my friend, Daryl, a mortal."

"A mortal!" Aghast he looked at Daryl. "Yes, I want to come, if I can help."

"You will, Vald. Let's go then."

The three friends left, followed by a frolicking Dick.

***

Night came down. Daryl's stomach was empty and growling. He hadn't eaten since breakfast. "I am so starved, I could eat a horse, man," said Daryl.

Vald gave him a worried look.

Paddy laughed. "It's just a way of speaking, for mortals." Vald's

15

eyes shone with relief.

"When we have found a safe place to sleep, we will eat," said Paddy.

"But with what?" asked Daryl.

"I know a good spot," said Vald.

After walking for a while, they reached a lovely meadow covered with sweet smelling clover and a bubbling brook running through it.

"All right! You have everything for a good meal, Vald," said Paddy, clapping his hands.

"Yes it's nice, but I cannot eat grass," whined Daryl.

"You haven't changed." Paddy chuckled. "It's wonderful to have you back." He gave a friendly slap on his chum's shoulder. "Here is your food."

A white tablecloth was spread on the clover with a splendid dinner. "Let's celebrate our reunion!"

Daryl's favorite foods were there. "Wow! Cool. How did you do that?"

"That is one of the elementary exercises you learn in wizard's school," replied Paddy, very proud of his training. "I am still learning. I am still too young to be a full wizard."

Daryl ate without any further questions, eyeing the desserts, his love. The young elf gave Daryl a big smile. He was so happy to have his friend and relieved that he had gone to earth before it was too late. Now his human chum was not about to die, and he could, once again, enjoy his company.

Full to the brim, Daryl talked excitedly until he was exhausted and he fell asleep. Vald and Dick by his side did the same. Paddy watched! He knew Xary would attack when they were not on guard. The young wizard's eyes flickered. He yawned. "I can cope with him," he said and then he went to sleep.

Xary's fiery eyes were observing the little group. Viciously, he sent an enormous salamander to kill them. The slimy tongue of the heavy beast moved toward Daryl. Quickly, it caught his foot and pulled the young mortal to its mouth. Daryl woke up kicking and screaming, "Let me go, let me go!"

Paddy jumped immediately to his feet and sent a bolt of lightning at the tongue. The pain was so intense that the salamander let go and turned its fury against the elf. The beast hissed furiously. Its tongue like a serpent darted at Paddy, who jumped from side to side to avoid it. The young elf threw bolts of lightning with no result. The hide of the monster was too thick, and Paddy's wizardry didn't yet have the strength and power of Niko's. However, he knew that every day his power was getting stronger.

Chapter 5

With the hissing of the beast, Vald and Dick woke up. The giant realized that Paddy was in trouble, getting weaker. Vald shook his fright, and head down ran to the salamander, ramming it, with one of his horns piercing the carapace. The monster caught fire and in a burst of flames was reduced to a pile of ashes. A howl of rage shook the forest.

"Thank you, Vald. I told you, you would help."

Shyly, Vald lowered his head.

"You heard Xary, Vald. He didn't like your work," Paddy said with a chuckle.

"Wow, what a battle, man. I am cheesed off that I couldn't help," said Daryl, angrily.

"You are in an another realm, man. When there is a battle, which is not often, the weapons are magic."

"Then I won't ever be able to help?" asked Daryl sadly.

"Yes, you will." In Paddy's hand appeared a slingshot. "I suppose you still know how to use it?" he said, laughing, "It's a magic slingshot."

"Do I remember, man? Wow! Wonderful! Xary had better stay away from us. Doesn't look magic to me," replied Daryl, looking at it closely.

"Take my word for it, it is. You'll see. It never misses."

"Wow, cool, thanks, man. Magic or not, I feel better with this in my hand." On earth, Daryl had been a champ.

It was now almost sunrise. They ate their meal and moved on. Vald continually looked around with big, worried eyes.

Paddy said, "The only way to destroy Xary is to go to his lair."

"Why?" asked Daryl.

"He will never come to us himself. He will always send his creatures."

"But, man, do you know where he lives?"

"No, only that he lives in the Forbidden Mountains."

"Have you been there?"

"Never."

"Wow! Aren't you presuming a lot of your ability, man?" teased Daryl.

All that time Vald had been silent, then he spoke. "I will guide you. I know the way. When I was a child I went into the mountains with my father."

They stopped.

Dick, facing his master, was listening, his shining brown eyes going back and forth from one to the other.

Paddy laughed. "Yes, boy, you are coming."

The dog jumped joyously.

"Dick is a good dog, Daryl."

"I know. He is to me as your Tiger was to you. Is he still alive?"

"Very much so, and as young as Dick."

"Wonderful! I loved that dog. I love you just as much, Dick."

Their meal finished, they left.

"We will have to walk the rope," said Vald.

"What's that?" asked Daryl with just a touch of fright.

"Oh, yes, I heard about it," replied Paddy. "It's made of entwined ropes and wood. It was constructed by the Dwarves to protect them against an Urk invasion. The Urks are much too heavy and so couldn't use it. It is secured between two mountains and crosses above a huge chasm."

"And you say we will have to use it?" asked Daryl, alarmed.

"There is no other way to reach the Forbidden Mountains," replied Vald.

"How did you do it with your father?" asked Paddy.

"Father is a Shaman. He used magic and carried me."

Daryl quivered and said, "I'm not looking forward to this experience."

"Come on, man, did you lose your nerve? You have always been more daring than I," said Paddy, giving Daryl a slap on the shoulder.

"I guess inside I am still a frightened old man. What about you, Vald? How are you going to walk it."

Vald's eyes shifted anxiously. "We'll see," he replied.

At the end of the forest they entered into rolling graveled hills with extremely poor vegetation. Paddy made a face. "Not too inviting." he said.

"You said it," replied Vald, "It's the land of the Goky. Nasty little people, lazy, thieves, and liars. They love to fight for no reason at all."

Dick growled, his hair stood up on his back.

"What's the matter, boy?" asked Daryl.

More growling. They looked around, and didn't see a thing. Vald said, "They are hiding, blending into the surroundings."

"Let's find us a spot to rest," Paddy suggested.

Daryl whined, "We haven't had anything to eat since this morning, man, and it's almost night."

"Oh, yes," said Paddy with a chuckle. "I forgot that your stomach is your faithful clock. Just wait a little longer, okay?"

Paddy ran to find a cave. Not far away was exactly what he was looking for. He entered with caution. All was clear and Paddy gave the signal to come. Once inside, they sat on the sand. The young wizard conjured up a good meal with clover and water for Vald. Then the elf organized the watch, Vald first, followed by Daryl, and then himself. They rolled into their capes, pulled their hoods down, and went to sleep.

The first part of the night went well. Vald woke Daryl, who, moaning and groaning, took his turn. The full moon gave a good view all around. Then, a large cloud appeared, covering the moon. Paddy woke and sat beside Daryl. Yawning, he whispered, "This is the perfect moment to attack us. Hush, don't move, they are approaching. Let them come closer."

Suddenly, lightning filled the sky, frightening the young human, who jumped. Then he realized it was Paddy's doing to give them light. The ground was alive with strange little creatures. Their small round heads were perched on top of a balloon-shaped body with tiny legs and arms. All wore brown-beige tunics, the color of the hills they lived in.

Daryl yelled, "They are footballs." Laughing, he ran to give a good kick at the one standing in front of him, sending the astounded fellow yards away up in the air. "Wow! I am going to have fun with these guys!"

"No, Daryl, they are nasty," screamed Vald.

For a while, the lightning stopped their advance. Soon the ignoble little crowd realized that it was harmless, and, buzzing like huge bumblebees, they attacked, shooting darts through hollow sticks.

"All right," said Paddy with a grin. "You want to fight? We will fight!"

Bolts of fire came out of his hands, making big holes in the ground where they fell in. Terrified, they had a hard time getting out of the small craters. They ran away escorted by Paddy's laughter and Daryl's kicks.

With a grimace of pain the human said, "Nasty little things! I have been stung by their darts, and they burn like fire."

"Their darts are coated with a sort of venom," said Vald. "If wounded enough times, you will fall asleep, and they rob you to the bare bone. They are too small individually, so they attack in big numbers."

Daryl's legs were swelling under his pants and so was his left arm with sausage-like fingers. "Nasty little things," he repeated. "How can I walk or do anything with these fingers?"

"I'll fix that," said Vald, sitting beside him.

"Do you have any salve or other medicine with you?" asked Daryl, now in real pain.

"No. Touch my horn with your hurt arm." The giant bent his head down.

Grimacing, Daryl painfully raised his arm and touched the horn. Immediately, the pain left the wound.

"It works!" cried the young human.

Vald bent down lower and touched Daryl's legs.

"Of course it does," said Vald, offended.

"Sorry, Vald. I didn't mean to doubt you and your power. I have to get used to magic."

Paddy restored the good harmony by cheerfully saying, "The Goky will not come again tonight. Let's sleep." Then, with a chuckle he said, "You haven't lost your touch at kicking a football, man?"

"Nope."

"We will leave the watch to Dick. Okay, boy?' Paddy laughed, patting Dick.

The dog barked, and sat at the entrance of the cave.

✳✳✳

The next morning after a good meal Daryl was completely well. The Goky had been badly frightened and were not in sight. The rough ground made their progress slow. Holes had been worn in Daryl's shoes, pebbles had found their way in. Disgusted he sat. Grumbling, he looked at his shoes, and lifting his foot, asked, "How am I going to finish the quest with shoes like this?"

The young elf laughed moving his hand. A splendid pair of brown elfic boots appeared.

Joyously Paddy threw them to Daryl. "Here, Daryl."

"Wow! Where do they come from, man?"

"Magic! Have you already forgotten that I am a wizard?"

"Well, not really. Things like that are not normal to me, Paddy."

Quickly he pulled off his old shoes, and cast them away. Laughing, he shouted, "For the Goky." Joyously, he kicked the dirt, dancing around with Dick barking.

Paddy explained to Daryl that his new footwear was special. "They are elfic boots. When it's cold they stay warm, and when it's hot they keep your feet cool. They have other advantages that you will discover as we go along. Now, let's move! We want to get out of these hills before darkness."

They plodded in this grim country for hours. The sun was getting low on the horizon when suddenly the ground gave way. The three friends and Dick fell into a deep pit. Daryl's human eyes couldn't see in the dark.

Chapter 6

Paddy and Vald had natural night vision.

"Where is Dick?" screamed Daryl as he fell past Paddy. Quickly, the young wizard grabbed him, slowing down their descent with magic.

"I have him with me," shouted Vald. He, too, used his power to prevent his huge body from crashing below on the rock. They finally landed in a large cave, which had a strong, rotten smell.

Daryl didn't dare move. Scared, he said, "It's pitch black, and it stinks."

Paddy reached into his doublet. "Just a minute, man." Quickly, he took Daryl's hand. "Here, take this stone. Think you want a bright light, you will have it. Think you want to dim it down, or extinguish it, and it will happen."

"Cool. This is wonderful! I love your realm, Paddy. Wow! What an awful place. I don't see any way out."

Vald replied, "Yes there is one." In long strides he left, with Dick in his arms.

"Stop! Don't!" shrieked Paddy.

"Why? It's perfectly safe."

"No! It's not! There are invisible things. I see them," said the boy. "You wouldn't survive the attack."

Vald, trembling, backed up behind Paddy. The young wizard raised his arms and threw strong bolts of lightning into the tunnel. The ground shook. Howling and a terrible stink filled the cave. Paddy promptly covered his friends with his cape.

"What's the matter, man?"

"The monsters have exploded like bags full of poisonous gas," replied Paddy.

"All right, but why the cape over our heads?" inquired Daryl.

"Nothing will harm us underneath it. It's an elfic cape. If you were an elf, you could see through it. It reacts like your boots. If the weather gets cold, it keeps you warm. If it's too hot, it keeps you cool. You also fly with it. It has lots of magic uses."

"Wow! I wish I had something like that," said Daryl enviously.

The young elf ignored his remark. Through his cape, he was looking intensely across the cave. Vald, with Dick in his arms, was crouched on the ground under the cape. The petrified giant hadn't said a word.

"What are we waiting for Paddy?"

"The gas has not yet dissipated," replied Paddy.

"How do you know that, man?"

"I can see the green fumes in the cave. We have to stay until they're gone."

It seemed to Daryl that they had been waiting for hours! His stomach was growling. "I am starved!" he whined.

Paddy laughed. "Okay, man." At the elf's thought, the cape pushed the gas away, enlarging into a big tent. Till now, they had been standing up, except for Vald. With a sigh of relief, they sat to enjoy their meal provided by Paddy. Tired, all went to sleep with Dick snoring.

* * *

Suddenly the dog woke, barking furiously with hairs up on his back. "What is it boy?" asked Daryl, waking up.

"Obviously, we have a visitor, and Dick doesn't like him," replied Paddy, now awake.

"Who is it?" whispered Daryl.

"Osha," replied Vald.

"Who's Osha?" asked Paddy.

"A nasty genie who lives in the hills and befriends the Goky," answered Vald.

"I wonder what he is up to," muttered Paddy.

"Perhaps he will be gone by morning," said Daryl and yawned.

During the night, Osha tried removing the cape. Each time he was brutally pushed away. All the tricks he knew were tried, including his enchanted dance, where he crowed like a rooster until he became red in the face and collapsed on the ground.

Through the cape, Paddy and Vald watched. The young elf chuckled. Finally, Osha gave up and went to sleep. Inside the tent, they did the same.

Much later Paddy woke up. Osha was nowhere to be seen. The young elf laughed. "I guess he has been quite humiliated. I don't think he will bother us any more."

Daryl stretched his arms, and alarmed by the preparations of leaving asked, "What about eating, man?"

Dick barked approvingly.

"Don't worry. You, too, Dick." Quickly, Paddy conjured up a big breakfast.

"Wow! Cool. Thanks. After a meal like this, I will be ready to fight the Sorcerer of the Forbidden Mountain and Osha," said Daryl, grinning.

Meal over, Paddy said cheerfully, "Let's go." With a sweep of his hand he removed the cape, threw it over his shoulders and walked to the tunnel entrance.

Daryl sighed taking his elfic stone out. If only he could see in the dark. For hours they went down crawling between rock formations. Then, they were in sandy soil, showing marks of heavy footprints strangely spaced far apart and covered with huge fetid pieces of dung that they had to jump over.

"I wonder what that means? I don't like it," said Paddy, very observant, for a fifteen-year-old elf.

Dick sniffed the strange thing and growled.

"He doesn't like it either," said Daryl.

The temperature rose. Vald grabbed Dick, who was panting heavily.

"Where are we going, man, to Hell?" said Daryl, and chuckled, wiping his dripping forehead with the back of his hand.

"It seems like it," replied Paddy who didn't sweat.

"Never been there. Never heard of it either," said Vald, curious.

"What? Oh, you mean Hell? Never mind," said Paddy, laughing.

As they rounded a bend of the tunnel it suddenly ended, overlooking a boiling crater. No exit was in sight. A terrible stink came from across the burning pit.

"Look!" whispered Daryl, terrified.

On the other side of the crater, facing them was a gigantic green beast, a sort of dragon, without wings. It had a long, heavy, body covered by scales as large as huge round table plates. It was watching them with shining purple, slit-eyes full of ire. The powerful hind legs were ready to spring and the beast's flat tail was switching from side to side with anger, raising a cloud of dust and gravel. The long neck, now stretched to its limit, was supporting a huge ugly lizard-like head showing sharp yellow teeth and a flicking black tongue. The beast's short front paws were anchored in the rock.

They froze. Daryl, shivering, said, "Wow! What a horrible looking creature. I am glad it's on the other side of that furnace."

"Don't be so cheerful, man," replied Paddy

"Why?"

"Remember the large prints in the sand and the droppings?"

"Yes, what about it?"

"That's it, man."

"What! But how?"

A terrible roar shook the cave.

"Look out! Run! Run!" shouted Paddy.

"We can't leave you here," cried Daryl.

"Do what I say! It's coming after us," shouted Paddy.

In a mighty spring from its hind legs, the monster leaped over the crater and landed where Paddy stood. The young wizard jumped back, greeting the beast with huge bolts of fire and lightning. Startled, the monster, roaring furiously, stopped for an instant, its enormous claws gripped in the rock. Paddy changed his tactic. Quickly, the young wizard bound the monster, like a package, with magic ropes. The beast lost its balance and with a loud cry fell into

26

the burning pit.

Vald and Daryl bolted into the tunnel.

Paddy, puzzled, said, "I wonder how come we came to that monster's lair?"

Shrill laughter echoed in the tunnel. "Osha," cried the wizard. "You almost had us killed." More laughter from the genie.

"You changed the course of the tunnel nasty fellow," said Paddy.

"You are clever for a so young wizard," replied a sour voice.

"Mind your own business, or you will regret it," said the elf.

They left backtracking.

After almost an hour of searching, Vald cried, "Here is where he meddled with the course of the tunnel. That nasty genie deals with the Goky, so why not with Xary, too?" asked the giant.

"Never mind to whom he belongs. Let's not fall for his tricks again," replied Paddy, angrily.

They progressed cautiously. The tunnel went upward. The intense heat was gone replaced by a pleasant temperature. A narrow plateau with an underground stream greeted them. Dick jumped out of Vald's arms, rushed into the stream, and noisily guzzled some water. Paddy and Daryl quickly removed their clothes to join the dog. Laughingly, they splashed Vald, who prudently stayed on the shore. Fun over, they got dressed and traveled silently for hours. The stream had disappeared into a hole. Then, Dick, hair up, sniffed the ground loudly.

"What is it boy?" asked Paddy.

Upon rounding the next turn the tunnel opened into a large cave where a party of Urks, crouched by a fire, were fighting.

"Daryl, douse your light," whispered Paddy.

Chapter 7

A deep darkness shrouded everything. Only the flames lit the savages' faces. The monsters had a poor sense of smell, which was very fortunate for the little party hidden in the obscurity. Quickly, they backed up.

Paddy let a soft cry out. "Look!"

"What is it?" breathed Daryl, frightened, hanging onto Vald's long fur.

"They have two prisoners," murmured Paddy. "But they are children!"

"Elfic children," whispered Vald.

Then Daryl saw them. Horrified, shivering, he murmured, "They are going to eat them!"

"Not if I can help it. Vald, keep Dick quiet."

The kind giant took Dick in his arms. The dog licked Vald's face showing he understood. Daryl still hung on to Vald's fur.

Paddy, cloaked with invisibility, disappeared to the sight of his friends. Quietly, he approached the terrified children locked in each other's arms. They looked at Paddy with big, terrified green eyes. With their elfic vision they could see the young wizard. Paddy put a finger to his lips and talked to them in the silent elfic language.

Listen, I will take your hands. You must not move. Do you understand?

Yes, their eyes replied.

Chapter 8

The Urks were engaged in loud laughter, playing a game of bones and screaming and fighting for a good place to sit at the banquet. They weren't paying attention to their little prisoners. Paddy took the children's hands and immediately they were cloaked and invisible.

The Urks, too late, realized the loss of their meal. They howled in rage, searched the cave, and left running by another tunnel looking for their prey.

Paddy and the children rejoined Vald and Daryl.

The elf curiously asked, "Who are you, children? You must have been far from your village. Usually, the Urks don't come near the houses."

"My name is Tony of the Third Realm of the Flying Elves," said the young boy, "and Sabrina is my sister. We were returning to our parents' house from a visit to our uncle, Lord Zorat of the Blue Mountains, when the Urks attacked our escort. They have now eaten them all, and we were to be the final feast. I thank you very much. The King, our father, will reward you handsomely."

"I know both your father and your uncle," replied the elf. "I am Prince Patrick of the first realm of the flying elves. King Ariol is my father. Do you know the way out, Tony?"

"Yes. Come Sabrina."

The little elf, trembling, held her brother's hand tightly. As they walked by, she gave a terrified look at the firepit, where a huge spit turned, with a pile of bones beside it. They ran across the cave where fumes of charred flesh lingered with the horrible odor of the Urks.

The obscurity promptly engulfed them in the dark mouth of the tunnel the Urks had taken. Daryl, still without light, hung on to

Vald's fur for dear life. The elf asked Tony to walk by his side and Sabrina by Vald, with Daryl.

The young prince haughtily replied, "I will not. I stay with my sister."

"Tony, it's for your safety," said Paddy.

"I am sorry, but I want to protect Sabrina," replied Tony, stubbornly.

Paddy ignored Tony's remark. "Sabrina, please take Vald's hand. Tony, stay beside me. Let's go before the savages realize we are just behind. They are not too far ahead. They have stopped. Do you know why, Tony?"

"I think so. This cave has a large waterfall. There, they meet with other bands of Urks to go hunting."

"Doesn't sound too good, man," mumbled Daryl, who had been mighty quiet.

"Stay here. I will see what's happening," said Paddy, cloaking himself.

Quietly, the teenage wizard left. After a short walk he found the band. Silently, he worked his way right into the group and stopped beside their leader, who growled, "We have to find the elves."

Hungry cries replied.

The leader yelled, "They can't be very far. Take the main tunnel, it's the only way out."

"Ya! Ya!" screamed the monsters, scrambling out into another tunnel. In the rush, as he came back to his friends, Paddy was almost trampled by the mob. He reported what had been said.

"They have taken the only way out." After a short pause to think, Paddy said, "Why not try the water. It must not be cold because of the volcano. We can see the steam."

"Good idea," replied Daryl, letting go of Vald's fur. He took his light out, and quickly he ran toward the waterfall. The sound was deafening, filling the cave.

Running beside Daryl, Paddy smiled as he remembered, "You were a mighty swimmer on Earth. You used to scare me stiff, man."

"Yup."

The cataract was very high. The young wizard sent a burst of light for Daryl to dive.

Paddy thought, It will be easy for the human, but what about the rest of us?

Vald had arrived and was visibly horrified by the gushing water. "I will never jump. I would prefer to be fighting an army of Urks!"

"I know, but there is no other way, Vald. Hurry before the light gives us away," replied Paddy.

"I can't swim!"

"I'll help you through, Vald," said Daryl.

Paddy, worried, turned his eyes to the children. Tony laughed. "It will be a game for us. We will fly down."

"I forgot that you were flying elves. Now, what about Dick?"

"No problem, man. Dick loves diving and swimming." Daryl chuckled.

"All right! Hurry! You go first and help Vald when he arrives. I'll stay here to encourage him to jump."

Daryl, followed by Dick, stood up on a rock, bent down, and with his hand touched the water.

Smiling, he shouted, "It's perfect."

He jumped with Dick, who paddled the air joyously with his paws. Both made a splendid dive. They disappeared in the turbulent waters and came back to the surface immediately. Daryl spat out some water and signaled Vald to come.

The giant at the edge of the rock was petrified with fear. Paddy used his magic and pushed him. Vald screamed from the top of his huge lungs. The young wizard's power helped him to come down slowly. Daryl caught Vald, before he went completely under and quickly brought the giant up to the surface.

"Good dive, Vald," said Daryl.

Huffing, puffing, sneezing, and spitting water, Vald said, "Paddy pushed me."

Daryl laughed. "Well, admit that you wouldn't have jumped."

"I know."

The children, stamping the rock impatiently, were ready. Tony opened his arms with his cape secured to his wrists and jumped. The cape, like a large wing, brought him down. Sabrina followed, and then Paddy. Horrible screams made them look up. Paddy quickly doused the light. The band of Urks was back howling like demons and throwing rocks at them.

"I can't swim," cried Vald.

Daryl held the giant's head out of the water, shouting, "Don't worry, hold onto my hips, and let yourself float!"

Rocks thrown from above were falling dangerously around them. They swam quickly away. Once out of danger, they settled down to a steady pace. They were in the water for hours.

Then Paddy shouted, "Vald, you can walk. It's not deep now. Try it."

Tony saw fear clouding the big brown eyes. "It's okay, Vald, don't be afraid," said the boy.

The giant took courage, put his feet down, and let go of Daryl's belt. The water reached his waist. Vald sighed.

"Listen, man," said Daryl

Chapter 9

"Yes, be quiet. Someone is pounding hard on rocks," whispered Paddy. The closer they approached, the louder became the noise.

Vald whispered, "See, there are flickering lights in the water."

"Hush! Stay still. I am going to have a look. Daryl, douse your light."

The elf, now invisible, moved noiselessly. A group of men with egg-shaped heads and strange gills on each side of their necks busied themselves pounding on pink and white stones, polishing them and carefully lining up the product of their work on the bank.

A dark green beard touched their bare chests. Long, shining, light green hair was tied in a knot behind their backs. Only a pair of yellow fisherman's pants covered their agile, slender legs.

Paddy watched them for a while then said, "They seem to be a peaceful bunch."

Quickly, he returned to his friends who anxiously asked, "What did you see?"

"Nothing alarming, just men working in the river. However, we should be prudent. We don't know if we are welcome here."

Paddy, Daryl, and Vald resumed their walk in the river. The children and Dick swam, the water being still too deep for them.

The workers stopped. Curiously they watched the small party arriving. A tall individual came forward. "Greetings, strangers. I am Yorg, son of Yarga, King of the Mirmids."

Paddy politely answered, "I am Prince Patrick, son of Ariol, King of the Elves of the Promised Valley."

"What brings you to our kingdom, Prince?" asked Yorg, looking at Paddy with large watery green eyes.

"I am on a quest and traveling with my friends. Pursued by the Urks, we took the river to escape their attack," answered the young elf.

"Yes, they are afraid of water. That is why we are safe here," replied Yorg.

"Will you show us the way out?" asked Paddy.

"Certainly, but first, come to rest for a while in my father's palace. We don't receive many visitors." Yorg put a crewman in charge and said, "Come with me, please."

They walked for a while. The water was now shallow and the river quite wide. Tony and Sabrina were splashing Dick and laughing. Then at the bend of the river, to their surprise, appeared a lovely pink sandy beach with children screaming and laughing as they played in the water. Curious, they stopped their games to look at the strangers.

Paddy, inquisitive, said, "But this is the same stone that you are washing! Why do you do it? You have so much here."

"There is no nutrition in this," replied Yorg.

"What do you mean. Do you eat this powder?" asked Paddy astonished.

"Yes, it's part of our daily diet. We would die without it," replied Yorg.

The children giggled.

"They are stone eaters," said Tony.

Seriously, Sabrina whispered, "They must be very heavy. That's why they stay in shallow water, otherwise they would drown."

Tony laughed. "You are silly."

Daryl joined the laughter.

Led by Yorg, the party waded out of the water followed for a while by whispering children, who soon returned to their games.

The party entered a large musty tunnel lit by torches secured on the walls and decorated with beautiful colored paintings of fish and water vegetation.

"This is a strange mural," said Paddy.

"It's marvelous, man," replied Daryl who loved the sea and all its inhabitants.

For the longest time they walked in this strange environment. Silently, one side of the tunnel opened, and two huge arms grabbed Sabrina. Terrified, she screamed. The wall closed.

Tony pushed the stone wall shouting, "Sabrina! Sabrina!"

Dick barked angrily and dashed to his master.

"What's the matter, boy?" asked Daryl.

Dick pulled his coat, barked, and ran back to Tony. The three men arrived where Tony was hysterically screaming and kicking the wall.

"What's wrong, Tony? Where is Sabrina?" asked Paddy and Daryl in one voice.

Short of breath, red-faced and sweating, the young boy told how his sister had disappeared.

"Yorg, do you know of any other beings living in these caves?" asked the young wizard.

"Yes, the fairies, quiet, gentle things. Sometimes there is Buloo, genie of the clouds, a huge, harmless fellow. He comes down at times to visit the fairies."

"Do you think one of them could have kidnapped Sabrina?" asked Paddy.

"I don't know," Yorg, baffled, said, "Let's go to see my father. Maybe he will have the answer."

They walked quickly in silence. Tony's joy was gone. Dick sadly walked beside him.

The party arrived in a large hall with lots of happy, oval-faced people, who immediately surrounded them and started questioning them. Yorg explained that they had an urgent matter to discuss with the King. A visit from outside was a great event for these gentle folks. Disappointedly, they opened a passage to let them by.

A continuity of beautifully decorated halls and corridors led them to a large door made of two huge pink shells. Yorg touched one, and it quietly slid open, revealing murals of strong, rolling white-capped waves and a sea full of multicolored fishes, corals, and all sorts of marine vegetation. They were in an immense artificial aquarium. In that strange room, pink and white granite seats were shaped like sea shells, and the floor was covered with a thick coat of fine gold sand, as soft as a woolen rug. The royal room was lit by gold torches resting upon turquoise pedestals in the shape of a dolphin. The far end wall was painted with huge transparent waves and had two gigantic white whales, one on each side of the royal throne, which was made of a huge abalone shell, shimmering softly against the wall, giving the wet impression of coming out of the sea.

"Wow, man! I wouldn't mind having a room of my own like this," whispered Daryl, mesmerized.

Prince Yorg smiled. "We are people from the sea. Centuries ago, our ancestors were attacked by monsters coming from the depths. Our only chance of surviving was to leave the sea and adapt. That is why we harvest the pink rocks. In those we find the things we need to remain alive out of the water. In memory of our beautiful lost kingdom our ancestors decorated the tunnels, caves, halls and rooms with the beauty of the sea."

A door on the right slid open, and a very tall man entered. Curiously, he looked at the visitors with a smile. A dark green beard brushed the gold collar of his green robe. Light green hair fell upon his broad shoulders. His large, watery, almond-shaped eyes stopped on each visitor. The resemblance with the prince was remarkable.

"Greetings, gentlemen, and welcome to the Kingdom of Mirmid,"

"Salutations, King Yarga of the Mirmid," replied the elf. "I am Prince Patrick, son of King Ariol of the First Realm of the Flying Elves."

"I am Daryl, a human from the Earth Realm of Ireland."

"I am Vald of the Valdos tribe."

All courteously bowed their heads. The King nodded his head each time with a smile. Then he looked at the boy. "And you, child. Who do you say you are?"

Proudly, the boy squared his shoulders, lifted his head, and looked the King in the eyes. "I am Prince Tony of the Third Realm of the Flying Elves."

Chapter 10

Suddenly, Paddy saw in his mind's eye, Sabrina screaming and kicking at the man who had thrown her over his shoulder like a bag of flour as he carried her away. Then, in the wink of an eye, the man and Sabrina were among the clouds. The genie (because it was Buloo) stopped to open a transparent door and then walked inside.

"Who's the genie living in the clouds?" asked the elf.

"It is Buloo, Genie of Clouds," replied the King.

"He has kidnapped Princess Sabrina, Tony's sister," said Paddy.

"How do you know?" asked the King, baffled.

"I am a wizard. Young, but still a wizard, King Yarga. I could see her," replied the elf, continuing watching inside the cloud. Paddy heard soft music and children laughing.

✳ ✳ ✳

Sabrina was so surprised that she forgot to struggle. The genie put her down. She turned to him, "Who are you? Where am I?"

"I am Buloo, Genie of the Clouds," he replied gently.

"Why did you take me away from my brother?" She began to cry.

"Don't cry, little one," said the genie. "You are here to be happy. Listen to the children." He opened a door. In the center of the room a huge golden carousel, full of boys and girls having a marvelous time, slowly turned. The music was enchanting, and Sabrina stopped crying.

The genie smiled, gestured, and Sabrina found herself on the carousel, riding a white unicorn with a shining gold horn. She started laughing with the children. Buloo sat in a large soft cloudy chair. Hands on his round belly he watched the laughing children.

* * *

"This is insane. I must free her," mumbled Paddy.

The elf watched Sabrina who tried talking to the other children, but no words came out of her mouth. Fear struck her. No tears came out of her eyes, and she could not stop laughing either. The genie was still smiling.

The little girl's mind was clear to Paddy.

Terrified, Sabrina sobbed without tears. "Am I going to stay here forever?" Her small shoulders heaved.

The other children were really happy. Paddy wondered why. Then he noticed that none of them were elves. They were of the other races from the Elfic Realm, but not elves. The carousel was enchanted. However, its power had no lasting effect on an elf. The genie didn't know that!

The carousel stopped. Joyously, the children stepped down and ran to the next room to eat. Sabrina followed and tried to talk to the children. They didn't give her a look, and no sound was coming out of her mouth. She cried with no tears. She was hungry, so she ate. Dinner over, the children ran back to the carousel, laughing, but still not talking. Broken-hearted, Sabrina followed.

* * *

The young wizard told King Yarga what he saw. Sadly, the King said, "Nothing like this has happened for years."

"But, it has happened?" asked Paddy.

"Yes. We never found the child."

The elf asked permission to leave, with his friends. He couldn't stay. He had to rescue Sabrina. They left the palace with a guide to show them the way to the surface.

Outside, the stars gave off a gentle light in the cold sky, and to their surprise at the horizon was a large puffy white cloud making a strange hole in the night. The guide bowed his head and quietly departed.

Paddy took Tony's hand. Both walked in the stillness of the night, Dick at their heels. Daryl and Vald were lost in their conjectures.

After a while a few trees showed their dark silhouettes against the sky.

"We better stop and sleep under the boughs of those trees," said Paddy.

The young wizard conjured a light supper and set spells around them.

All rolled in their capes and went to sleep. Dick curled up beside Tony.

The boy had a restless sleep and awoke when his keen elfic ears heard crying. Quickly, he went to Paddy. "Prince Patrick, Prince Patrick," he whispered.

"Yes, what is it, Tony?"

"Listen. I can hear Sabrina crying. It's coming from the sky! It's crazy!"

"Not so, Tony. Hush, please." Paddy listened. "Yes! It comes from that big white cloud. Your sister is with the Genie of the Clouds. You found Sabrina, Tony."

"But how are we going to get her out of there?"

"Leave it to me. Go to sleep."

✽ ✽ ✽

In a large dormitory, Paddy watched the children going to bed with no laughter. A disoriented Sabrina, looking around, found an empty bed.

In the middle of the night, Paddy's voice whispered, "Sabrina, we found you. Our camp is almost under the cloud. Listen, tomorrow, when you get off the carousel, don't follow the children. Leave the same way you were brought in. When you get out, fly down. I will shield you. The genie won't see you. Good night, Sabrina."

Next morning found Paddy watching the girl. She was one of the first to be up to wash. Quietly, she looked around. The genie was nowhere to be seen. The little elf went to the carousel with the children. A few minutes later the genie walked in and sat in his comfortable chair, looking at the children with a smile. Paddy whispered, "Smile, Sabrina, or soon you will be crying."

Sabrina climbed up on the carousel, laughing like the others. A few hours later the carousel stopped, the children went to eat. The genie left the room. Sabrina slowly walked to the door by which she had entered the first time. Freedom was just across the hall. She ran, opened the outer door, and jumped, spreading her arms. A huge hand came out of the cloud to seize her.

"Oh no!," she screamed, terrified.

She realized she was still coming down. The young wizard had been faster than Buloo. Sabrina, shielded by a powerful spell, couldn't be seen. She was safe. Gently, she touched down.

Paddy whispered, "Stay where you are. Don't move. The genie can't see you."

Sighing, she sat.

With big tears rolling down his chubby face, Buloo walked by. Sabrina locked her arms tightly around her knees. The genie stayed for a while, turning like a hound dog. Finally, he left sobbing.

* * *

About that time, her brother and friends showed up. The children fell into each others arms, crying for joy. Dick, overjoyed to see Sabrina, performed his best greeting dance around her.

"I am glad, Sabrina, that you didn't move. The genie couldn't see you. I am going to shield you both with a special spell. If Buloo tries to catch you again, he won't feel your bodies."

"How weird! How is this possible, man?" asked Daryl.

"Wizardry, man."

Paddy touched the children. "Now you are invisible to the genie."

"But I don't feel any different," said Tony.

"Never mind. You are. Let's go," said Paddy. "We have a long way to walk."

The day was gray, and the large cloud above had a black, stormy color. Buloo was unhappy.

After several hours they arrived in a valley of small round mounts full of briars and thorns.

"I don't like this place," said Daryl.

"Neither do I," replied Vald.

The young wizard remained silent, watching the sky where heavy dark clouds gathered. A cold wind started blowing.

"Bad weather is setting in," said Paddy. They covered themselves just in time. The rain poured down.

"Vald, can you see any shelter?" asked Daryl.

"No."

In the distance the thunder rolled and it became even darker.

"We had better find a place to stay. I wouldn't like to have us going any farther in such weather," said Paddy.

The wind was extremely strong, so strong that the children had a hard time moving on. Paddy took Tony's hand, and Daryl helped Sabrina. They approached a copse.

Vald said, "There is a large bush at the base of that mount. I am going to open it for you to crawl in."

"But there won't be enough room for you," said Tony.

"That's all right. I don't mind the bad weather. My fur is good protection," replied the giant.

Paddy didn't want to leave Vald out in the storm. He moved his hand shielding the giant from the fury of the elements. Satisfied, the young wizard rolled in his cape. Dick curled up under his master's cape and snored. Paddy was happy to have Daryl with him, just like on earth. For a while he listened to the storm raging outside and soon drifted asleep.

✳ ✳ ✳

Paddy and Daryl jumped up. A terrible crash of thunder and lightning had wakened them. The whole valley was ablaze. Vald was fighting lightning bolts, which were being thrown at his head. Fiery arms were trying to get his horns. Paddy looked up to see where the attack was coming from. "Oh, no! I forgot to protect Vald against the sorcerer!"

In the sky large red eyes were focused on his big friend. Vald's magic horns were automatically responding to the attack. Terrified, he had the hardest time staying up on his huge legs under the brutal onslaught. Fire was all around him. The elf sensed Vald's tiredness. The sorcerer was waiting for the moment when his victim would fall. Then, he would cut out the horns from his head, and probably kill him.

The young wizard furiously attacked the evil one, sending powerful bolts of lightning right into his eyes. Enraged and blinded by the elf's fire, the sorcerer answered, missing every time. Paddy kept up his attack until Xary left, beaten. The thunder growled in the distance but the wind had died down. Exhausted, Vald had fallen to the ground where he lay still on his back. Daryl ran to him, making sure that he was not dead. Paddy took out his bottle of wonder water and gave him a drop. Vald fell asleep right where he was.

The children hadn't awoken. Daryl went back to his cape with Dick beside him. Paddy shielded Vald and stayed by his side in case Xary decided to come back and finish the giant.

✳ ✳ ✳

The morning was still wet with heavy rain. The adults didn't talk about the fight, which had occurred during the night. Paddy spread his cape over them like a huge tent and used his power to set a feast. Vald also came inside, enjoying his vegetarian meal.

"If we don't find a proper shelter tonight, we will all sleep under my cape."

Breakfast over, Paddy gave the signal to depart. "Tony and Sabrina, you are going to sit on Vald's shoulders," said the elf.

"Why? We can walk," replied Tony, offended.

"Thank you," said Sabrina. "It will be fun, Tony, I will be able to see a long way."

"You can, if you like to, Sabrina. You are a little girl, but I won't," said Tony, showing anger in his voice.

"I am sorry, young man, but you will. The briars are too high now, and we could lose you," replied Paddy sharply.

Sabrina was already on Vald's right shoulder, giggling. Then she said, "Dick is too small, too. He could be lost."

Vald chuckled and grabbed the dog. "Come on, Dick. I will carry you."

"Oh, thank you, Vald," She leaned down and gave him a kiss.

"Up you go." Vald grabbed a grumpy Tony, sat him on his left shoulder and walked away. Daryl smiled. For the gentle man-beast, those three were like flies.

The weather was still dark and wet but the wind had died down. The ground had changed. Vald, aware of the bog he was entering, warned Paddy and Daryl of its depth and danger.

"I am glad to be up here on your shoulder, Vald. Thank you," said Sabrina.

Dick barked his approbation, but Tony kept a sullen silence. He hated being treated like a child.

Vald smiled. "You are welcome, Sabrina." He patted Dick's head.

Paddy and Daryl now were in water up to their belts. Vald was only in to his ankles. The cold water was seeping into their boots and clothes, but being elfic raiment, they dried immediately. Their progress was extremely slow because of the terrible conditions of trampling in the bog.

"I don't know how much longer I will be able to walk like this, man. For sure, not too long," said Daryl.

Paddy turned to answer and fell face down in the muck. Before the eyes of his friends, Paddy disappeared. Quickly, Daryl dived. They did not come up.

Chapter 11

Vald quickly gave Dick to Tony. "Hang on to my horns, children." The giant bent over, plunged his huge arms into the water and started rummaging through the tall weeds.

The hole where they had fallen in was very deep. At last Vald found them, tightly bound by weeds. They were unconscious, drowning. Vald grasped one in each hand and pulled. A strange force was holding them captive. After a mighty yank, they bobbed up to the surface.

Paddy coughed and spat out a lot of water, but Daryl, being mortal, remained extremely pale. Vald carried both of them to where the water was shallower and put Paddy down. Daryl was still limp in his arms. From his pocket, Paddy took out the wonder water and forced a bit between Daryl's lips. Soon his color came back. He opened his eyes, surprised to see his friends looking at him so intently.

Paddy joyously said, "Good! Welcome back to the land of the living. How do you feel, man?"

"As if I had been hit on my head by a big stone."

"Okay. Let's get out of here, then."

Vald helped Daryl to his feet. The young wizard cast a spell, sparks encircled the group, and they were out of the bog.

"Wonderful," cried Tony. "Please, put me down, Vald."

Dick barked, jumped from Vald's arms, went to his master lying on the dry ground, gave him a slobbery smack, and started to run. Everybody laughed.

"I think, Tony, that you were not the only one who didn't appreciate Vald's kindness," said Daryl.

"Oh, but I did," said Tony turning red, "but…"

"I know, I know." The giant laughed.

Daryl was not yet too strong, so they decided to stay and camp. Nothing hospitable was in sight, and dark heavy clouds were again rolling in the sky announcing the rain.

"We won't stay under my cape. We all deserve a good rest." The young wizard moved his arm. A strong, tall cabin appeared. Vald would be comfortable.

Sabrina ran into the house, crying with delight. A large fireplace burned brightly. Paddy had even thought of setting a table with a pot of beef and vegetable soup. The delicious aroma tickled everyone's nose. Vald had food waiting for him as well. Cheerfully, they sat down and ate.

After supper, warmed by the hot soup, they all sat around the fire to enjoy the heat. Too tired to chat, they soon got into bed. Vald had a thick mattress of straw on the floor.

Paddy had protected the house with strong spells. Only the sound of the crackling fire in the chimney and the pattering of the rain as it beat the roof were heard.

Soon, thunder and lightning joined the rain. The wind started howling, too, around the house. Paddy woke up feeling the sorcerer's evil presence outside. Lightning hit the house and bounced off with no damage. Xary screamed in rage. Paddy turned over and went back to sleep, leaving Xary to his frustration.

✳ ✳ ✳

Morning. The weather was still bad. Paddy let the children sleep in. No point to take them out in the storm. The young elf produced a good breakfast.

The aroma of hot chocolate woke Sabrina. Quickly, she jumped out of bed and ran to the table and licked her lips looking at the croissants. Vald had a large bale of sweet clover.

A loud, "Wow!" resounded into the cabin. "Splendid, man! Splendid!" cried Daryl. The young human sniffed the eggs, sausages, bacon and hash browns with delight.

45

"You haven't changed, Daryl," said Paddy, laughing.

"Nope! I still love to eat, man"

"We are stuck here for a while," said Paddy.

"With food like this, I don't mind a bit, man," said Daryl, his mouth full.

"Hooray!" The children jumped, accompanied by Dick's barking.

Paddy threw a damper on their enthusiasm. "Sorry, we will leave as soon as the weather clears up."

The sorcerer was getting bolder and closer. Last night he had caused a raging storm. Breakfast over, the adults sat by the fire and the children unleashed their energy by running around the room. Dick followed, barking his head off. Paddy had to put a stop to the noise. Dick, sighing, went to sleep beside his master.

Late in the afternoon, the wind died down, and the rain stopped. The sky was still heavy with crawling dark clouds,

"We will spend the night here," said Paddy.

Of course, everybody loved the idea. The warmth and the security of the house was great. After a nice meal and quiet games with Dick, the children went to bed, while the teenagers and Vald talked by the fire.

In the wee hours of the morning, Dick woke. A strange noise made him grumble. Paddy jumped to his feet. With hairs standing up on his back the dog growled louder.

"What's wrong, boy?" asked Paddy.

A long arm was coming down the chimney. Slowly, the hand approached Vald's head. The giant at once felt the evil waves. Quickly, he grasped the arm in his huge hand and twisted. A terrible cry of pain pierced the night. Xary tried furiously to free himself

During the night, the fire had died down. Paddy blew it into immediate life. The flames jumped high and bright. Another sharp cry came from the roof.

The elf said, snickering, "Let him go, Vald. He will leave us alone for a while now."

Vald released his grip. The evil one, screaming in pain, took his arm out.

Daryl had been watching, absolutely fascinated. "Wow, man, I am glad you are a wizard." Quietly, he returned to his bed.

One hour later, Paddy said, "Wake up everybody! Let's eat, and go."

Breakfast over, the young ones ran outside. A few clouds still lingered in the sky. Paddy and Daryl shivered. Dampness gave them a disagreeable cold kiss, and they quickly pulled their collars tightly around their necks. Paddy gestured, and the house disappeared. Tony, Sabrina, and Dick splashed joyously in the puddles from the night. The desolate look of the country had nothing to cheer their spirits.

"I wonder where the sorcerer's lair is?" pondered Paddy.

Vald replied, with a sullen look, "Quite far from here. It will take us a long while before we get there."

"I am glad you know where to find him," said Tony.

"Are you sure? We won't get lost somewhere?" asked Daryl.

Paddy laughed. "Don't worry, man. We will find it. Don't forget that Vald has been there once with his father."

They trod over rocks and thorns for hours. Daryl was grateful for his elfic boots.

Daylight faded, and they moved into the mysterious twilight. Night was almost at hand. Paddy looked for a cave.

"Why don't you create another house for us, man?" asked Daryl.

"To have power is a great privilege, Daryl. One must never abuse such a privilege. Emergency is the key. Let's find a place to camp."

Tony promptly left.

"Wow! Now I understand. You could use your power and go directly to the sorcerer's lair without us."

"Right, but in the end I would lose out. I wouldn't have gained anything in courage, knowledge and friendship."

Tony, running back, arrived. Beaming, he cried at the top of his lungs, "I've found a large cave!"

Paddy said, "Let's see the place." In long strides he left and quickly came back. "Good show, Tony. We will be well protected from the wind."

Darkness prevailed in the cave, so the human took out his elfic stone. Inside, they found big rocks, perfect to sit on. Paddy conjured food, and they ate. The meal finished, they rolled in their capes. Dick crawled in with Tony, and soon all was quiet.

Paddy, restless, got up and searched for a place to hide that he might observe the area without being seen. He looked up and spotted, high above, a large platform half way down from the ceiling. Quickly, Paddy flew up and sat. There, he could see and not be seen.

The elf felt the sorcerer's hatred in the cave and heard approaching, crawling in the tunnel, a creature probably created by Xary. Promptly, Paddy shielded himself with a strong spell and gave Vald a mild jolt.

The giant shook Daryl. The human took his elfic stone and his sling out. From above, Paddy zapped the gigantic gorilla as he entered the cave. The beast was covered by a leathery carapace and had two huge stingers poised on his forehead.

The strong bolts of lightning had no effect whatsoever on the heavy brownish skin. The gigantic beast walked straight up to Vald. Its growling was deafening. The monstrous stingers moved, ready to strike. Vald was terrified.

Daryl scooped up a big stone, put it in his sling, swung it around, and let it fly straight for the beast's eyes. It let out a terrible cry. One of its eyes was gone. Vald quickly grabbed the stingers in his hands and tore them off. Then, with a powerful blow of one of his horns, he pierced the monster's side. It burned with a horrible stink and became a pile of ashes. Once more the sorcerer was beaten. His rage shook the hills.

A heavy silence fell upon the cave. The children were still asleep. Dick had growled once or twice. Paddy came down from his perch. "You are a great warrior, Vald, and you too, man," said the young wizard, slapping his human friend on the back.

"No, I was terrified," said Vald.

Chapter 12

"So was I, Vald. The real courage is to act in spite of your fear," replied Daryl, wiping his forehead with the back of his hand.

Paddy said to his pal with a chuckle, "When I was on earth, man, I often desired to have that splendid courage of yours."

Daryl smiled, and said, "Let's go to sleep. Thanks just the same, man."

Silently, they rolled in their capes.

In the morning, breakfast over, they were ready to leave. Nothing was said to the children about the events of the night. They left the dreadful place. The weather had turned bad again.

"When is this terrible weather going to stop?" asked Daryl.

"We are in the Sorcerer's land, Daryl," replied Paddy.

Trudging on, they pulled their hoods over their faces. The children and Dick, walking head down, were silent. It took several hours to cross the hills. The gale had stopped blowing. From the top of a big rocky hill they could see below a large lake encased between dark green pines, like a jewel in its box. Four large black birds quietly hovered above it.

The distance to the lake was great. They walked a long time before reaching the shore. The children were exhausted, and even Dick didn't bounce around. They ate in silence and went to sleep under the boughs of a huge pine.

During their sleep the branches quietly closed up, making an enormous green bowl. The young elf woke up feeling that something had changed. Stupefied, he looked around. He was lying on silk cushions in a green transparent bubble. Through it, he could see the lake with the soft moonlight brushing the dark, calm waters.

Paddy didn't feel any evil influence. Only peace and quiet was about.

He whispered, "What a strange and lovely place. I wonder just where we are? I'd better go back to sleep."

Sabrina awoke, surprised to find herself on a soft bed, with a beautiful large, stuffed doll dressed in lace, silk, and ribbons beside her. The doll had golden hair, and green eyes like her own. The doll had a gentle smile. "Wake up, Tony. Wake up," she cried.

"What's the matter? Why are you shaking me like that?"

"Look, look around," said Sabrina.

"Bless my soul! Where are we?" Tony yawned.

"I don't know. Perhaps Prince Patrick will."

A little bit scared, she hugged her doll and immediately a surge of joy filled her heart. The children walked to the wall and looked outside. The sun sparkled gold on the waters of the lake.

Gently a bell chimed in the room. At once Paddy woke up, followed by a stupefied Daryl and a scared Vald.

"Where are we?" asked Vald and Daryl in unison with rounded eyes.

"Honestly, I don't know!" Replied Paddy, watching Dick sniffing around, but not growling. "We are in a friendly place. Evil forces are not around. See Dick. He is completely at ease, only curious."

"You are right, Prince Patrick," said a deep voice, coming from above. All looked up. No one was there.

"Where are we? Who are you?" asked Paddy.

"I am Treo, Lord and Master of the Green Forest, Lord of Peace and Light. You are guests in my castle. Welcome."

"Yes, of course. I know of you," said Paddy. "You are one of the four Great Ones among the wizards."

"You are right, young wizard. Now, please, come to me."

The ceiling opened, and a flight of stairs came down. Paddy led the way, followed by his friends. The stairs took them up inside a huge tree trunk.

On the landing an old man smiled. A long white beard covered his chest. Silky white hair fell on his shoulders and back, touching his

50

waist. A loose shimmering green gown floated on his tall, thin body. Gold sandals shone softly on his feet. An enormous emerald ring flashed on his right thumb.

"Welcome, young Prince Wizard, son of King Ariol, Flying Elf of the First Realm. I was your host a long time ago."

"Yes I remember. But your name was…"

"I have many names, young prince. Greetings, Vald, of the Valdos tribe. Greetings, Daryl, Earthly Man. Welcome, Prince Tony and Sabrina, elves of the Third Realm of the Flying Elves, nephew and niece of my good friend, Lord Zorat from the Blue Mountains."

Dick whimpered softly.

"Pardon me, Dick, Faithful Dog of the Earthly man. Welcome."

Sabrina was hugging her doll in her arms. "Thank you, Lord Treo, for the nice gift. I love her."

"You are welcome, child. She will love you, too. How are you going to name her?"

Sabrina's large green eyes shone as she said, "Amie, because she has been given to me by a friend."

"That is very nice, Sabrina. Thank you. She will always be a comfort to you. Don't lose her, child. Come in, please."

A door opened into a large empty hall where servants passed by silently. Lord Treo went to a very high door, which opened by itself. They were in a room above the forest canopy. The outside walls were made of what looked like thin crystal.

The castle had been built on a large platform made of huge intertwined branches. Through the windows they could see beautiful suspended gardens. Soft music came from the forest itself, filling the air with peace, harmony, and light.

Lord Treo invited his guests to sit on sofas as soft as clouds. Their feet rested on a thick rug. "Now, my friends, tell me your story."

Vald started saying sadly, "Your Lordship, Xary the Sorcerer is after my horns to increase his power."

"Yes, I know Xary and his wicked purposes. Now I understand your quest. Many times he has tried to attack me. His power is nothing against mine," said the great wizard with a chuckle. "That is probably one of the reasons he wants your horns, Vald. But to destroy me, he will need much more than that."

The giant lowered his head and said, "I am so scared. I had such a quiet life before, and now, I live in fear, hiding or fighting him. It's terrible."

"You are not alone, Vald. I am with you and so is Daryl," said Paddy.

"This adds to my sadness. Your lives are constantly in danger because of me," replied Vald.

"Don't be sad, Vald. Before we met you in the forest, my father, the King had sent me on a quest, to destroy Xary. Remember?"

The Great Lord Wizard said, "Vald, you have done well. I will reinforce your power in such a way that Xary won't be able to kill you."

Majestically, the Lord stood up in front of Vald, who was sitting on the floor, and raised his arms above his horns. Sparks came out from his fingers to encircle the giant. Vald appeared to be on fire! Then, suddenly, everything stopped.

"There, my friend. Nothing can prevail against you to take your life. Go in peace," said Lord Treo.

"But I don't feel any different," said Vald.

Lord Treo smiled. "You are. Take my word for it."

Many servants were moving about quietly. Lord Treo had asked for breakfast for all. Daryl, not daring to say a word, was famished and the food was welcomed by all. When they had finished, Lord Treo took his guests to his beautiful suspended garden. Vald, for good reason, excused himself and stayed behind. They walked across light bridges, going from tree to tree. Large branches had been made into flowerbeds cared for by young elves.

Sabrina delightedly talked to her doll. "Look, Amie, how beautiful this is."

Tony laughed, shrugged, and said to his sister, "You are silly, Sabrina. She can't understand. She is just a doll."

Sabrina was shocked and with tears in her eyes, replied, "But she does! I know she can understand me." Sabrina didn't know that she had an enchanted doll

"You are right, child," Lord Treo gently replied. "Keep talking to her. She loves it."

They went back to the palace where the old wizard invited them to stay and rest for a while. They didn't see Lord Treo again until the night before their departure. "Good evening to all. I see that you are ready to leave my home."

"Yes, your lordship. With your permission, we will leave early tomorrow morning," replied Paddy.

"That is well, my friends. Good night." He left in a haze of green vapor.

❊ ❊ ❊

The next morning, Lord Treo joined them for their last meal in his palace. When came the time to depart, the old wizard turned to Tony. "I have a gift for you, my young prince." He searched in his large pocket on the side of his long gown. "Here it is." In his hand was a simple whistle.

Tony looked at it with surprise. "A whistle! What do you want me to do with it, Lord Treo?"

Chapter 13

The wizard smiled. "You will do plenty with it, Tony. First of all, it doesn't make any sound, and it is a magic whistle. When you need something righteous, blow, and you will get it. If it is futile, you won't get anything. Each time you use it for things of no value it will lose a bit of its power, until it becomes useless."

"Then, I will have to think twice before using it," said Tony soberly.

"Precisely, my young friend. It will be a great teacher for you to learn to think before acting,"

"Thank you very much, your lordship. I will be wise."

"Good boy. Now, farewell."

Suddenly, they were on the shore of the lake. The large tree was still there. Sabrina ran to look underneath it. She giggled and said, "If I didn't have Amie, I would think all this was a fantasy."

On the shore a large boat was tied to a rock.

"This is very fine for us, but what about Vald? How is he going to go across?" asked Tony.

"That indeed is a problem. What do you think, Tony?" The young elf looked the boy in the eye.

"I don't know." Tony, baffled, stared at the lake.

Paddy said nothing to help.

Suddenly, the boy cried, "I know. I know. I am going to use my whistle. I will wish a big boat for Vald."

Tony took the whistle from his pocket and blew on it, wishing for a boat. "Here it is!" he cried excitedly. "Here is your boat, Vald."

Paddy smiled. Of course he could have done it, but he wanted Tony to practice using his power wisely. "Good show, Tony," said

Paddy. "Let's go now."

"I love this realm, man," said Daryl. "Magic, magic, magic everywhere. I love it."

Tony was very proud to be the hero of the day. The weather was nice with only a few clouds rolling in the sky.

"We will be on the other side soon,' said Daryl.

"I would like to think so, but I don't think it will be that easy," replied Paddy.

"It's nice to be in a boat. I love it," said Tony joyously.

"Not me. I don't like it," replied Sabrina.

"You never like what I like, anyway," said Tony, vexed.

Even though they were rowing hard, Paddy could see that they were making little or no progress. Vald was getting further and further ahead. When he stopped rowing it took a long time to catch up.

"Look, Tony, the four black big birds are back flying over the lake," said Sabrina.

"I see. So what? Birds usually fly in the sky, don't they, Sis?"

Vexed by her brother's sarcastic remark she cuddled Amie and didn't answer.

Paddy, too, had noticed the return of the birds. He stopped rowing and observed them in silence. Daryl continued pulling hard on the oars, but even with his efforts, they were not yet in the middle of the lake, and Vald was quite far ahead. The giant was waiting for them.

Suddenly, clouds covered the entire sky, and the wind rose, making the temperature drop. It became chilly enough for the children to put on their capes. The boat began to bob, much to Tony's delight and Sabrina's fear.

"The weather's getting bad, man, and we are a long way from shore," said Daryl.

Paddy, staring at the sky, replied, "You are right, and I don't like those birds hovering above us. They are too large for my liking and comfort."

Just as Paddy finished talking, the largest of the birds was hit by something. It screamed as it fluttered its way down, trying hard to stay in the air. Paddy realized that it was Vald's doing. They never saw the birds diving on Sabrina and Tony. It happened so fast that Paddy couldn't react.

The girl screamed.

The other bird seized Tony, who fought like mad, yelling, "Let me go! Let me go, you monster!"

The largest of the three birds, which had miraculously recovered, dropped one of its sharp claws on Paddy, grabbing the collar of his cape. Its other claw snatched Daryl, and it flew away with the two young men. A loud cry of triumph resounded.

Paddy realized that Xary was doing it to get them away from Vald's boat so Paddy couldn't succor him. Vald saw it all and could do nothing to help. The lake had started to boil. All his gigantic strength was necessary to prevent the boat from turning over. A terrific jet of flame burst in the giant's face, and he quickly dove into the bottom of the boat.

Then an enormous dragon stood up in the lake, blowing fire at him. A voice said in his ears, "Vald, he cannot kill you."

"He can burn me to cinders, for sure."

"No," said the voice, "but you can destroy him. Get up. You will see."

Dead scared, trembling, Vald, stood up in the boat. The furious dragon opened its mouth, letting go a jet of fire at him. Amazed, Vald didn't feel the heat. Vibrations like he had never felt before shook his horns. From their points lightning came out, zapping the dragon everywhere. Vald was ablaze, surrounded by fire, the dragon by lightning. Soon, an especially strong bolt reduced the monster to ashes.

Chapter 14

The lake became quiet and the wind died down. A cry of rage shook the forest around the lake. Vald looked up. His friends were still in the grip of the birds. The sorcerer had not let them go. With a burst of lightning from his horns, he destroyed them. The children flew down by themselves while Paddy helped Daryl with his power to glide to their boat.

"Thank you, Vald," said Paddy.

"What a battle," said Tony with admiration. "You are a great warrior, Vald."

"Oh, no. I am not. I was helped by Lord Treo."

"How?" asked Sabrina, still hugging her precious doll. "I didn't see him with you."

"He was there with all his powers," replied Vald. "I couldn't have done it by myself."

"Never mind. You did it, and that is good enough for me," said Tony.

"Thank you," replied the gentle giant.

Paddy and Daryl rowed in silence while Sabrina fell asleep, cuddling Amie. Tony bravely tried to be like the men and stay awake. But bit by bit his eyes closed, and he too fell asleep with Dick at his feet.

Stars were now shining in a deep blue sky. The two young men were terribly tired and still far from shore.

"We must rest. Let's call Vald and tie our boats together," said Paddy.

The giant rowed back to join them. "I am going to put strong spells around our boats. Then we will sleep in peace." Vald, exhausted, went to sleep immediately.

* * *

The next morning, they woke up, rocked by gentle waves. Daryl claimed he was being starved. Paddy conjured a good meal. The young elf released the boats from their spells and Dick barked excitedly.

Daryl laughed. "All right, boy. You asked for it." He grabbed the dog and threw him overboard.

"Oh, no," cried Sabrina. "Poor Dick, the water is cold."

Dick was splashing and swimming to his heart's content. Daryl let him play for a while, then picked him out of the water. Back in the boat he shook himself and sprayed everybody.

Tony laughed. "Good boy. Come on, fellow." He took his elfic cape and rolled the dog in it. A few seconds later, he was dry.

"Those capes are the most wonderful things I have ever seen, man," said Daryl.

An hour later they were close to a landing place, and they jumped into the shallow water and waded ashore. On this side of the lake, the trees were widely spread, and it was easy to see between them. Soft moss covered the ground. The wildlife was plentiful and unafraid.

"See all those little rabbits hopping around, and the squirrels chattering in the branches. Aren't they nice?" asked Sabrina.

The children frolicked with Dick, who was mostly interested in the rabbits.

"Don't even think about it, naughty boy," said Sabrina to the dog.

Stung by the reprimand, he let his head and tail down, but soon forgot about it and ran with Tony.

"Dogs and children are meant for each other," said Daryl, laughing at the sight. The two friends talked freely, enjoying each other's company, while Vald continually looked around with big worried eyes.

After several hours of walking in this peaceful forest, they stopped and Paddy conjured up a good meal. Everybody ate to his heart's content, and Vald forgot his problems for a while. The children tried to have Dick play with them, but he was too full.

"Up! It's time to go," cried Paddy.

"What a pity, man," said Daryl.

"Too bad, but we have to get on with it. Xary doesn't rest. Look at Vald. The poor fellow is so anxious to go," said Paddy.

Whining and complaining, the children moved on.

In the late afternoon they arrived at a large meadow with a brook running through. Two magnificent does and one fawn were drinking from it.

"Oh, look!," said Sabrina softly.

"Stay here!" Daryl commanded Dick, who was ready to have some sport with them.

"They are not scared," said Tony.

"They need not be," replied the young wizard. "They are the fairies of this forest."

"Oh, how do you know that?" asked Daryl.

Chapter 15

"I just know. I am a wizard. I can detect simple things like that."

"Simple things? Are you joking, man?" asked Daryl, stupefied.

"Night will be here soon. This is a perfect place to rest," said the young elf.

"But, what about the fairies?" asked Daryl, a little preoccupied.

"So, what about them?" replied Paddy.

"Won't they mind us?" answered Daryl.

"Oh, no. They won't. I talked to them."

"How, man? I didn't see you doing it," said Daryl, shocked.

"From mind to mind, elfic talk," replied the wizard.

"I can't believe it! You are pulling my leg, Paddy."

"You still have much to learn about me, man." Paddy chuckled.

"I can see that," replied Daryl, looking at the elf in an uneasy manner.

"They are gone," whispered the human, looking at the brook.

"I prefer that. I was uncomfortable knowing some fairies were watching me." Daryl laughed nervously.

"All right, let's eat, man, and you will forget all about it," said Paddy with a chuckle.

Already Daryl's mind was on the delicious food Paddy would conjure. The meal over they were ready to go to sleep.

The earth shook and cracked. Slowly, on the other side of the brook, a beautiful crystal tower rose, and a dainty bridge crossed the clear water. Two lovely young ladies were standing upon it.

"Welcome to the Forest of Peace. I am Mya."

"And I am Lys. Please come to our palace to rest."

Daryl, scared, jumped, and quickly said, "No, thank you. I prefer to sleep outside." Then he mumbled, "Don't trust fairies and, even less, things coming out of the ground like that."

"As you wish," replied the smiling fairy Lys.

"Why? Come, Daryl, it will be fun," said Paddy.

Grumpily Daryl replied, "Prefer to sleep here, man."

"I will stay with you, Daryl," said Vald. "Dainty things are not for me."

The young elf and the two children left with the fairies. Dick disapprovingly barked, and Daryl worriedly watched them go. He turned to Vald and said, "Man, I don't trust those fairies, and neither does Dick."

"Well, my feelings are the same," replied the giant.

Daryl mumbled and rolled himself in his elfic cape, still worrying about his friend and the children. Vald was restless and Dick lay beside him and whimpered.

Paddy watched a beautiful crystal door from the tower slide open in front of the fairies. Gold chandeliers without candles gave light to the hall, and a gentle tinkling of crystal bells filled the entire palace. The floor under foot was soft as clouds.

"What a strange and lovely palace," said Sabrina, hugging Amie.

"I don't like it," whispered Tony.

"Well, for once, I agree with you," murmured Sabrina.

Paddy was silent.

Mya escorted them to their rooms. They climbed up and up and arrived in a hall with several doors. Mya opened one, inviting the children to enter.

"Please, we wish to stay with Prince Patrick," said Sabrina politely.

For just a second, the fairy had a flash of anger in her eyes, and then replied sweetly, "Why, of course," and showed them to a larger room.

When the fairy was gone Tony whispered, "Look, Prince Patrick, there are no windows."

"Yes, I see that. It's late. Let's go to bed. We are all tired."

They washed in the beautiful gold basin and went to bed, falling immediately asleep.

The young wizard sat in a chair, concentrating all his energy as he probed the tower with his mind. What he found infuriated him. From the two talking fairies he learned that they were prisoners. But why?

Again, he let his mind search the palace to reach the room where all the fairies sat talking. He had the surprise of finding that there were three younger ones who had joined Mya and Lys. He listened intently.

"Pia," said one of them. "We have found the perfect mate for you."

Excited, she asked, "Where is he?"

The other two, much younger, giggled.

"In the golden room with the children."

"The children? What do you mean, sister?" asked Pia.

"He has two young elves with him. He is a prince. The children are prince and princess, too, but of another realm."

"What are you going to do with the children?" asked Pia.

"I do not know, yet. Maybe change them into goldfish for the brook. We will see."

The younger fairies giggled.

Paddy heard one say, "How fun!"

"And if he does not want to marry me?"

"You are so lovely, he will, my dear. I have lots of tricks up my sleeves. He will be yours."

Paddy was horrified. They had to get out before the fairies could act. Quickly, he began casting spells around himself and the sleeping children so the fairies could not read his mind. Then he woke up Daryl.

"What is it! Where are you? What? You are speaking in my head. I think, man, I am going crazy."

"No, Daryl. You can hear me. Listen. We are prisoners of the fairies."

"I knew those dames were up to no good. Why did you go, man?"

"H…Never mind. I want you and Vald to be ready to leave at any moment. I am going to fool the fairies. We will have to be very fast."

Paddy woke the children. "Hurry, Tony, Sabrina. We are going to escape. Don't ask any questions, just get ready in silence."

Before they left, the young wizard placed spells in their room, sending the fairies the waves of their presence. With his power he unlocked the door of their chamber. Quickly, they went down the stairs. In the entrance hall the crystal bells chimed frantically. The wizard stopped them with a sweep of his hands, erasing all unwelcome sounds. It took a little while to break the spells on the door and then they were outside, running across the bridge to their freedom.

Vald took the children, put them on his shoulders, snatched Dick in his hand with Daryl, and they left, running as fast as they could. Dick, sensing the danger, didn't make a sound.

They ran and ran for hours, finally leaving the edge of the Forest of Peace to enter the Green Hills. Now the fairies couldn't touch them. Panting, Vald dropped Daryl and the children and Dick. They sat without a word.

"I knew those dames were up to no good, man."

Sheepishly, Paddy said, "I guess I let my human side take over. I made a big mistake not to be repeated," the elf said soberly.

"That was exciting," said Tony.

"I am famished. Wow! It's good to be alive man. I want a good breakfast, please. Great emotions always give me an appetite."

Paddy laughed heartily. "Emotions or not, you are always hungry."

On the green grass a large rug appeared with a real feast on it. Paddy, still laughing, asked, "Is that enough for you, man?"

"Yes, yes!"

Dick barked with approval.

"Don't bark like that, boy," said Paddy, chuckling. "You are not going to eat as much as yesterday. You have to walk. Vald won't carry you, boy."

Dick whined.

Paddy, while eating, told his friends of the fairies' plot.

"Wow. How lucky you were, man," said Daryl, teasingly with his mouth full and his mischievous eyes shining. "Husband to a fairy! What do you want? A princess?"

"Be quiet, you bad egg." Paddy laughed.

Everybody was in excellent spirits. "We have lost enough time. Let's continue with our quest," said Paddy.

"Hoorah," said Tony. "More adventures."

Chapter 16

Vald was not so enthusiastic about the prospect of new adventures. They left following a river, which wound through the hills. Tony said he would like to go fishing.

"Sorry, boy, we are not on a fishing party," said Paddy.

Tony walked away sulking. Absently, he took his whistle out of his pocket and blew on it. Suddenly, he found himself seated on the riverbank, a fishing rod in his hands and his friends far ahead of him. Aghast, he mumbled, "I didn't ask for this?"

"Tony," called Paddy. "Hurry. You are going to lose us."

"Help! I am stuck. I can't move! " The boy tried to get up,

The elf left his friends and ran to Tony. "What's the problem? Why don't you come?"

"I can't move."

"What do you mean, you can't move?"

"I don't know. I tried and tried. I can't."

"I suspect Xary has something to do with it," said Paddy. "Give me your hand." The elf took Tony's hand and pulled, but he too was bound to the ground by a strong force.

Chapter 17

Meanwhile, a huge man dressed in rags and looking like something out of the Stone Age, had appeared and attacked Vald and Daryl. The thing had claws the size of daggers, which wounded Vald twice. Daryl swung his sling and the stone hit the monster's head between the eyes. It staggered. Then Vald blasted him with powerful bolts of lightning, and the man bolted away howling with pain.

At that instant, Paddy felt the force holding him gone. Tony jumped to his feet and ran to Sabrina who crouched on the ground with the doll pressed against her chest. Worried, Tony asked, "Are you alright?"

She nodded her head. "Yes," she answered in a shaky voice.

"Vald, Daryl, are you hurt?" asked Paddy.

"I tell you, that thing had terrible weapons on the ends of its hands," said Daryl, as he looked at Vald.

"Thank you. Your sling gave me time to get my wits together and strike back," replied the giant.

"I see you don't need me," teased Paddy. "Tony was the bait for me. The sorcerer tied me down. I fought him. While you were scared, Xary borrowed your strength from your horns to keep me tied down. Once Vald started using his own power, the battle was over, and I was free. You are a real knight, Daryl."

"A knight! Gosh! I remember on earth, man, when you were a kid, running down the road coming from the cliffs, yelling, 'I am a knight, I am a knight!' I thought you were crazy, and now it's me who wants to scream it." Daryl laughed, all excited.

"Well, things don't change very much, do they?" replied Paddy, smiling at his human chum.

"Nope, except when you take me to your realm to fight sorcerers and monsters," said Daryl with a chuckle.

While talking with Daryl, Paddy threw his elfic cape over Vald. The cape took the size of the giant, covering him from shoulders to toes. The poor fellow was badly hurt. A few seconds later the cape had healed his wounds. Vald, like new now, felt as strong as before the battle.

"Thank you, Prince Patrick, for giving me such a gift."

"You are welcome, Vald. Now, how are you, kids?" asked the elf.

"Well, thank you," replied Tony.

"Then let's leave this place. We have a long way to go," said Paddy.

"Yes, I have seen enough of this river," replied Daryl.

"I don't want to go fishing any more," said Tony gloomily.

Dick came out from behind a bush, where he had been hiding. "Here you are, brave heart, courageous friend," said Daryl sarcastically.

Dick whimpered pitifully and walked away, his tail between his legs and his ears down.

"All right, all right, you are forgiven." Daryl couldn't stand seeing his dog that miserable.

Dick, turned around, jumped at Daryl's face and kissed him. The children laughed and clapped their hands. Dick knew now, for sure, that he was completely forgiven.

* * *

The evening was cold. They walked for a long time before Paddy decided to stop in the hills and camp. Exhausted, Sabrina flopped on the ground, half-asleep. Dick curled up beside her. Tony would have loved to do the same, but his pride was at stake. Wobbling on his legs, he stood up until Paddy had set up a nice hut. Quietly, they walked in.

The meal was short that night. Amazingly, Daryl, for once, was more interested in sleeping than eating.

Paddy cloaked the house. Dick's soft snoring lulled everyone to sleep.

Morning was bleak. A high wind blew from the north. The sky dragged heavy clouds full of rain and snow over the mountains.

Sabrina sobbed, "I want to go home."

"What about you, Tony, do you want to go, too?" asked the elf.

"No! I don't want to. She can go if she wants. Anyway, she never wants to do like everybody else," said Tony grumpily.

Paddy reprimanded the boy, "Come on, be kind. She is younger and a little girl. The journey is hard on her."

This reminded Daryl only too well of his sister. Paddy quickly glanced at his friend with a twinkle in his eyes.

"I am sorry, Sabrina, your brother doesn't want to go," said the young wizard.

"He can stay. I don't mind," said Sabrina, crying.

Paddy then noticed the doll on the ground. Quickly, he picked it up and put the doll in Sabrina's hands. Immediately, the girl smiled and her tears went away. Sabrina forgot her longing for home.

"I am hungry, man. How about a good breakfast?" asked Daryl.

Paddy laughed. No one mentioned the incident with the girl. Dick was begging for food, going from one to the other, enjoying every bite of it.

"Enough, boy, you won' t be able to walk," said Daryl.

"Oh, poor Dick. But he is still hungry," said Sabrina.

"He is always hungry, Sabrina, just like his master," said Daryl with a loud laugh.

Sadly, the dog went to lie down by the door, his head between his front paws, watching to see if by any chance someone would have pity on him.

The children, now happy, watched the falling snow through the window. Soon they left and, to their misfortune, the snow had turned into ice pellets, stinging their faces. Quickly, they pulled down the hoods of their elfic capes.

Paddy didn't dismiss the hut, leaving it to be of use to some travelers or shepherds. Vald's heavy fur coat protected him well against the freezing gale.

The hills, now very rocky, were slippery and hard to climb. The prickly bushes, covered with shining crystals from the frozen rain, were an eerie sight.

They did not go very far that day since the wind was bitterly cold. They had to camp in the frozen hills. Daryl looked for a cave.

"Don't look any further, Daryl," yelled Paddy against the wind.

"Why? I will check behind that hill."

"No. Come back. I am going to provide a house. The weather is too nasty."

The young wizard moved his hands above his head. At once, a nice stone house appeared, with a good strong plume of smoke coming out of the chimney. Sabrina ran and opened the door. At the center of a large room was a round pit of stones with a fire burning high. A copper hood went up through the roof to take the smoke out. Around the room, nice comfortable beds with chubby feather quilts waited for them.

Sabrina with her doll dashed for one and she let herself fall, disappearing in the feathers, whispering, "Thank you, Prince Patrick."

"Dinner's served," cried Paddy.

Nose up, Daryl savored the delicious aromas. Now, lighthearted, he said, "Let's leave the bad weather outside forever, man."

The wizard made a circle above his head. "There, the house is protected by strong spells. This will make it impossible for the sorcerer to hurt us."

"Wonderful. You think about everything, don't you, man," said the young human.

"Not always. Remember the fairies? I didn't that time. It won't happen again."

Laughing, they sat at the table and ate in silence. All were too busy eating to talk, even Dick.

Once the meal was over, they all sat around the fire. Paddy and Daryl recounted to the children their times together in the Earth Realm. They laughed a lot, especially Sabrina and Tony, when Daryl told about all the mischievous things he had done to his mother's cat and his sister, and roared with laughter when Paddy told the story of the carrot patch, dug up by Tiger in his mother's vegetable garden.

"Where is your sister, Daryl?" asked Paddy.

"She passed away, many years ago. She never married. I don't have any family."

"You have us, man. Good night, everyone," said Paddy, falling on his feather bed.

As soon as their heads touched the pillows, Tony and Sabrina were asleep. Vald was by the fire with Dick beside him. The wind outside howled, and the fire crackled.

Once during the night the sorcerer tried to get at them, but Paddy's spells were too powerful to be broken. Furious, he caused boulders to roll down the hillside to crush the house. He made the wind stronger. Everyone in the house was sound asleep. Paddy awoke and felt his presence. The young wizard sent a powerful jolt at Xary, who screamed in pain. Paddy chuckled. The remainder of the night was quiet.

During the night, the wind had gone down and snow had been falling on the hills. Winter had shown its luxuriant cold, white coat. In the house it was nice and warm. When the little party woke up, the fire still burned high.

The youngsters looked out the window and screamed with excitement, "We have snow."

"Let's hope you will always feel that way," said Paddy.

"Oh, yes, we will." They clapped their hands.

"We'll see that later on," replied Daryl, smiling.

The children ate quickly, anxious to romp in the snow. Twisting on their chairs, they looked at the elf.

Paddy laughed. "Okay, you may go out, but stay near the house."

"We will, thank you," said Tony.

Dick barked enthusiastically.

They opened the door and dashed out. Tony grabbed a handful of snow and threw it at the dog.

After a while Paddy called them, "I don't like to be a party pooper, but we have to leave."

"Oh, so soon?" asked Tony.

"Yes, boy," then to Vald and Daryl, "Are you ready?"

"Yes, we are coming."

The young wizard moved his hand, and the house vanished. Just as soon as he did this, the wind began blowing, and the snow twirled frantically around them. However, with their elfic boots and capes they were nicely warm. The cold wind was biting their noses, and the young elves quickly pulled their hoods right down over their faces. Tears froze on Daryl's face.

Paddy asked him, "Why don' t you pull your hood down?"

"How will I see? I am not an elf, man."

"Try it," replied Paddy.

"You really want me to break my neck, don't you?"

"Don't argue, man, do what I say."

Daryl sighing pulled the hood over his face. Wonder of wonders, he could see through it. Stupefied, he asked Paddy, "How can this be?"

"I made it be," replied Paddy, chuckling.

"Thank you, man. How nice to be warm."

At noon, they looked for a shelter to have a bite to eat. They found a bush large enough to protect them against the wind. They sat nicely warm under their capes. Dick crawled under his master's cape. On Daryl's lap a hot dish of food appeared. Vald had a warm dish of hot oatmeal with molasses. Dick had his own food beside him in a bowl under Daryl's cape. Paddy's and the children's capes became teepees above them.

Daryl whined, "How do you eat with that cape? I am starved and can't eat."

"Oh. Poor you. Think of your cape as being a teepee, and it will become one."

"I can't do things like that, man."

"Try it. You will see what happens."

Without conviction, Daryl did it. At that instant the cape extended, the hood moved up above his head in a perfect teepee shape to protect him and Dick. "Wonderful! It worked!"

"I know," replied the elf. "Trust me, when I tell you things like that, man."

Daryl didn't reply. He was eating.

71

Chapter18

The snow now fell heavily. Vald was constantly shaking the snow off himself. Paddy realized his friend was having a hard time. Silently, he moved his hand in Vald's direction; then, a very large teepee covered him, too.

"Thank you, Prince Patrick."

"We will stay here until the snowstorm is over," said the elf.

"I think I will sleep," said Daryl.

"Good idea, but before you do that, I will protect our little camp with a cloak of invisibility."

The teepees now were completely buried under the white snow.

Tony talked mind to mind with Paddy and Sabrina. "I will be with Vald."

"All right, Tony."

Much later, it was still snowing heavily. "I think we are here until tomorrow!" shouted Paddy. "We will be more comfortable in a house." The young wizard moved his hands, and they were in a warm room with a fire burning in a large fireplace. Soft, puffy seats were in front of the fire. Beds, against the walls, bulged with feathery quilts. At the center of the room, a large table had a steaming hot meal. The teenagers sat talking by the fire. The children ran around the table with Dick barking.

"May we eat, please? We are starving," asked Tony.

Daryl said, "I thought you would never ask. My stomach was worrying."

The children fought for a morsel. Paddy stopped them, and to their great disappointment, took the piece for himself. Dick ate to his heart's content. He drank, sighed, and went to sleep. All were ready for bed. Paddy cloaked the house. The snow outside continued falling gently.

In the dark night, small shadows walked by, sniffing the air. Their cruel brown eyes looked all around, searching for something they knew was there. The goblins' long pointed noses could smell the presence of the elves. Ferociously, they searched round and round. It was fortunate that Paddy had cloaked the house. In the wee hours of the morning they tired of searching and left, still looking back, hoping to see the elves somewhere.

Paddy's mind had been aware of their visit and was watching, ready to act.

In the morning, the snow had stopped falling. The hills were covered with a thick fluffy white coat; the wind had died down. Tony and Sabrina were up and ready to play in the fresh snow.

"May we go outside for a while, please?" asked Tony.

"Yes, Tony, but we had visitors last night, the goblins. Stay close to the house, you hear me?"

With screams of joy, and barking from Dick, they bolted outside. Paddy quickly walked to the door. "Not so much noise. We don't know how far they are." He closed the door.

Vald, concerned, said to the elf, "We must be extremely cautious. Winter is setting in. The bands of goblins are returning for the season to the deep caves of the high mountains."

"I don't like those creatures. They are mean," said Paddy.

"I am calling Tony and Sabrina for breakfast," said Daryl.

"Yes, the weather is good, and we must use it," replied the elf.

The children came in, and once breakfast was over, they all left. The human boy could feel the danger around, but his mortal senses were not as sharp as those of his friends. The children and Dick were quiet.

Around noon, the elf's keen ears caught sounds coming from behind the hill they were about to climb. Immediately, Paddy grabbed Dick and gave him to Vald. A finger to his lips he stopped the little party. "Hush," he whispered.

Quietly, Paddy left. Almost at the top of the hill, he crouched down and began crawling on his stomach. A whiff of smoke brushed his nose. On the other side a large band of goblins were laughing and fighting around a fire. Quickly, Paddy crawled back and swiftly ran to report the bad news.

He whispered, "We must get away from here, pronto. There is still a chance to escape detection, but if the wind changes and blows in their direction, we have a problem."

"Wow! I wouldn't give a penny for our lives then, man," Daryl grimaced.

"You said it, friend," whispered the elf, "Let's go."

The little party changed direction, heading for another trail. Tony whispered, "The wind's up and blowing toward them!"

Paddy said, "Run! It won' t take long before we have the band after us."

He was right. Screaming, goblins emerged at the top of the hill.

"Hurry, Vald, take Dick and put the children on your shoulders!" shouted Paddy bolting through the snow.

They ran like the wind (elves run that fast). Vald, in gigantic steps, followed without any problem, but Daryl was far behind, trying desperately to catch up to his friends. Vald realized Daryl's difficulty and halted. Quickly, he put Dick under his left arm, and, when the young mortal arrived, the giant scooped the poor panting Daryl, and as he resumed his running, shoved the human under his right arm.

The screaming goblins were almost at dart shot range. Vald with no great effort put a fair distance between them. The goblins howled in rage as their prey was getting away.

The elf and Vald ran until they were completely out of sight of their enemies. The giant knelt and let his grateful passengers down. Dick jumped to the ground, shaking himself.

"What's the matter, boy'? Don't tell me Vald gave you fleas," Daryl said and laughed. Shocked, the dog looked at him and walked away.

They sat to clear their minds.

Paddy said, "It's a fact, the area is infested with goblins. Now, no noise, no laughter, and Dick, no barking. We will walk as silently as pussy cats."

The children giggled. "Pussy cats," they murmured.

The elf talked to Dick, eye to eye, and explained that he had to stay silent.

The dog whimpered.

"Good boy."

"Did you talk to Dick, man?" asked Daryl.

"Yes, I did, and he understood perfectly."

"Talking to my dog. You are pulling my leg, man," grumbled the young human.

"Let's move, before the goblins catch up to us," said Paddy.

They walked in the direction of the high mountains. A bitterly cold wind blew at them. Quickly, they pulled their hoods over their faces and returned to the trail they had left the day before. Hours later, they found a small plateau with frozen shrubs and icy rocks. The wind there howled like a lonely wolf

"It's not a very nice place, man," said Daryl.

"No, but we will have to make do with it," replied Paddy.

"I guess so." Daryl didn't like the howling. It gave him goose bumps.

The wizard conjured a small sturdy log cabin, with a cheery plume of smoke coming out of the chimney. "Sorry, Vald, you will be a little bit cramped, but I couldn't make it bigger. If a group of goblins were to pass by, we don't want them bumping into our house."

"Don't worry, I can sit by the fire."

Once inside, the young wizard cloaked the cabin. It was warm and cozy, with the cheery fire burning, spitting sparks joyously. A good hot meal was spread on the rustic table. Daryl forgot all about the sinister howls and attacked the food with gusto. The meal was quiet. Exhausted, they went to bed.

During the night, a little light flickered from bed to bed and decided to stop on Tony's. It stayed there for the longest time, not disturbing the boy's slumber. Dick opened an eye and in one leap tried to catch it.

"What's the matter, boy?" asked Tony, drowsily. Paddy woke up. "What's wrong, Tony?"

"I don't know. Dick jumped on me."

The elf looked Dick in the eyes. "He says a small light was on your bed. When he jumped to catch it, it disappeared."

"He must have had a bad dream. Maybe he ate too much last night. Now go to sleep, or I will kick you off my bed, understand?"

Eyes full of reproach, head down, Dick curled up at Tony's feet, with a big, "Hmph."

As soon as they were asleep, the little light came back. This time it played on Tony's nose. The boy woke at once. "What's this?"

A small giggle replied.

Tony tried to catch the light with no success. It was too fast for him. The more he tried, the faster the light went. "Leave me alone," he whispered, "I want to sleep."

The little light left. Tony, now grumpy, dropped his head on the pillow.

In the morning he told Paddy about the light. "What was it Paddy?"

"It's a young mountain genie who wanted to play with you. Okay, let's be ready to leave after breakfast," said the elf.

Not a crumb was left on the table. Regretfully, they walked out into the bad weather. The wizard dismissed the cabin. A strong, freezing wind buffeted them unmercifully. Walking was difficult. The narrow trail had been trampled during the night by a horde of goblins, leaving tracks leading onward.

"It's fortunate we have the wind blowing from the mountains. The goblins won't know we are on their tail," said Paddy.

"Let's hope it stays that way," replied Daryl.

"Yes. If one of their darts were to hit me, it would be disastrous for us. The poison they are coated with would neutralize my power."

Chapter 19

"You mean, gone forever, man?" asked Daryl, worried.
"Yes. My only chance to regain my power would be to get the ring from the old Gremlin's finger.

"Where does he live?" asked Daryl.

"Far away, in the Granite Mountain," replied Vald.

"Wow! Better not have a fight with them," said Daryl.

"Precisely, man," said the wizard.

Now aware of the double danger they faced, they moved as shadows in the cold stillness of winter. They didn't dare to stop. Elfic biscuits, with snow to drink was their food. Only Vald had his big bale of clover, which he ate along the way, and Dick, like everyone else, had elfic biscuits. The trail wound along the mountain and the giant more than once almost fell into the abyss.

Paddy was concerned and said, "Vald, I can provide elfic boots for you."

"No, thank you. I don't think I could walk with them."

In the high mountains, darkness arrived suddenly, and they still had a long way to go before reaching a safe place. The trail became even more hazardous. Paddy watched the giant.

Sharply he said, "Vald you are going to try those boots. They will help you a lot in the dark. Here, put them on, please," asked Paddy.

"But…" Vald turned around to answer, his foot slipped, he lost his balance, and tipped over into the abyss.

"Hurry, Daryl. I need you to stop him. You know how to use your cape, come." Paddy jumped in the abyss.

The young Earth boy hesitated just a split second and flew beside the elf murmuring; "Can you see him, Paddy? I can't, man." Daryl's human eyes couldn't pierce the heavy falling snow. The veil was too thick.

"Yes, I do."

"Okay, I see him now."

"Fine, go to his left and grab his arm."

"Gotcha, friend," said Daryl to Vald.

"Hang on, Vald, we are going up," said Paddy from the right.

The children and Dick, looking down, were very still, spellbound. The young human and the elf breathed with relief as they helped Vald to set foot on the trail.

Tony looked at the formidable footwear standing like towers beside him. Seriously, he asked, "Are you going to put them on, Vald? Or do you prefer to plunge into the ravine again?"

The giant sighed without answering, and put them on.

Tony with a grin asked, "Well, how are they?"

"Fine. I don't feel them. They are so light," replied Vald amazed.

Paddy whispered, "Good, let's go. We want to be comfortable tonight. We deserve it."

Vald walked as if he had nothing on his feet and didn't miss a single step. "This is wonderful," he said to Daryl. "Thank you, Prince Patrick."

It was pitch black when Paddy found a huge cave. He left to check for enemies. When he came back, he announced, "We will sleep in there. The goblins have already been here. I have enough room for a small cabin. You will have to sit down, Vald."

"I don't mind."

They entered the cave, the wizard twisted his hand, and a small log cabin appeared. "Let's go in. We won't have a fire. The smoke would give us away. But I will put spells at the entrance of the cave. The goblins won't smell us, or see the cabin."

Vald bent down to enter in. A spell of warmth made the place comfortable. They were so exhausted that even Daryl didn't look at what was served. Without a word, they went to bed and slept almost instantly. Dick, that night, chose to sleep on his master's bed. Tony was sound asleep when the little light tickled his nose. "Oh, no! I am so tired." He opened his eves.

A giggle answered.

"Enough! Why don't you show yourself, instead of hiding in that silly light," said Tony, angrily, sitting up on his bed.

The small light became a large gold bubble. Tony was flabbergasted to see inside, a smiling young boy dressed with baggy yellow pants. He was bare-chested. From the top of his bald head a long dark braid of hair hung down to his waist. His large brown eyes, full of laughter, looked at Tony.

"Who are you?"

No reply came from the boy, but through the bubble came his hand. Tony took it and found himself inside with the boy. They flew outside in the sky, way above the clouds of snow. Then, the bubble separated in two and Tony was in his own bubble, zipping from star to star, playing hide and seek in the winter sky with the young boy. The stars disappeared, and Tony found himself in his bed.

An hour later he got up. Stretching his arms, he said, "Prince Patrick, I had a lovely dream last night."

"I know, I watched you," said Paddy.

"How could you? It was a dream!"

"No, it was not. I am always aware of any magic around me, Tony."

"What do you mean, magic?"

The young wizard ignored the question, because the rest of the party had awakened. They ate a good breakfast.

Outside, the wind had died down. The weather was clear and very cold. Paddy erased all trace of their presence, including scent. Silence was still in order.

They climbed up and up for the longest time. The cold was so fierce that even Vald's heavy fur was not protecting him. Paddy and his friends kept warm with their elfic capes. Sympathetically, the young elf watched Vald shivering. The poor fellow was freezing.

"Here, Vald, put this on," said Paddy.

"I never put anything on."

"I know, but this will keep you warm."

"I wonder what I will look like with boots and cape," replied the giant fellow with a chuckle.

"Never mind what you will look like, Vald," answered Paddy.

Vald grumbled between his teeth and put the cape on. Immediately, a feeling of warmth came over him. A little ashamed, he said, "I must apologize, prince. This cape is wonderful. I am warm all over. Thank you."

"What a strange character this giant is," said Tony to his sister.

The trail abruptly turned sharply to the right, and led over the top of a large frozen waterfall by way of a huge rope net, tossed in the wind. The ice shone like a piece of metal under the gray sky.

"It's beautiful," said Sabrina.

Daryl looked at the thing dancing a dangerous ballet in the gale. Unlike Sabrina he was not impressed by the beauty of the site. He saw only danger, and fear struck him.

"Yes, it is Sabrina," replied Vald. "I will walk across, I am not going on that flimsy thing. It will break under me."

"All right, we will meet you on the other side, then," replied the elf.

Tony, always ready for adventure, quickly said, "I will go with you, Vald."

"I think it's better and safer for you to go with the others, Tony."

"Oh, but it will be fun to walk on the ice," he replied disappointed.

"And dangerous, too," said Paddy.

The giant left with Dick in his arms, and the rest of the party headed for the huge net.

"Vald would have torn the net for sure," said Sabrina very seriously.

"Yes, he is a mighty big fellow," replied Daryl.

The human gingerly put his feet into the net. Afraid of falling through, he moved very prudently. He clung onto the rope on each side and advanced carefully. Tony and Sabrina followed, laughing. They ran, making the net swing and bounce.

"Stop that!" screamed Daryl, petrified with fear. "It makes me sick!"

The children giggled and stopped.

In spite of its solid appearance, the ice broke under Vald's heavy weight. He got wet feet, but immediately his magic boots dried them up. They all arrived safely at the same time. Vald put Dick down. The slippery trail remained narrow, continuing to go up. Dick missed his step and fell into the deep gorge.

"Dick! " screamed Daryl horrified.

Tony daringly jumped after him. The dog was going down like a stone! The boy hurried to catch him before he crashed at the bottom and killed himself. Finally, Tony was beside him.

Tony jokingly said, "Hi, boy! Want a ride?" He caught the dog by the nape of his neck. The problem now was how to take him up. The young elf needed his arms to fly, and right now, both were falling fast! Quickly, he placed Dick around his neck like a fur collar. The dog understood and anchored his front paws firmly on Tony's chest. They flew up safely to the path.

The young wizard had watched the boy carefully, ready to jump down in case of need. This was Tony's doing. The young elf didn't want to take his pride away.

They arrived sound and safe warmly greeted by all. They cheered quietly because of the presence of their enemies. Sabrina jumped up and down, and kissed both brother and dog. Tony was the hero of the day.

Daryl bent down to hug his dog and said, "Be careful, little friend. I don't want to lose you. "

Dick licked his face, his simple way of saying "Thank you."

Paddy looked at Tony and smiled, the young elf grinned back. The teen wizard thought, One day the boy will be a fine elfic knight. Vald took Dick under his cape.

The little group continued its way up. It was completely dark when they arrived at the summit. A pleasant surprise awaited them, a large mesa. Paddy brought back the big stone house Sabrina loved so much. The fire was burning high in the fireplace. The beds were ready, and the table set. To Sabrina, it was like coming home.

The children sat quietly around the table, eating in silence. There was no giggling, no fighting for a special morsel. Even Dick made no fuss beside Daryl. All were very tired, overwhelmed by the events of the day and conscious of close danger. The emotions had been draining. Sabrina fell asleep at the table. That evening only the young men and Vald talked by the fire.

Paddy cloaked the house to render it invisible. Soon the only noise was the crackling of the fire and a gentle snoring from Dick, who, that night, had chosen to sleep with his hero, Tony.

During the intensely cold night, a long black line of goblins arrived on the plateau.

The leader became very excited. His pointed nose up in the air, he let out a long howl. "Elves! Elves!" he cried.

Chapter 20

The young prince wizard had seen them arriving. He watched for a while and unconcerned went to sleep.

The group stomped the ground, frantically searching. Furious, they screamed in rage. They couldn't find the elves. For hours they tramped around. Because of the magic set by Paddy, they were pulled away from the house. Finally, they left in a state of extreme frustration.

Tony was sound asleep when the little light flickered upon his nose. Dick was so tired after his odyssey that he didn't wake up. Paddy, aware of the Genie's presence, watched the boys in his sleep.

Drowsy Tony said, "Hi! I would like to play, but I am really tired."

The little genie smiled and gave him his hand. Tony found himself in the golden bubble, flying in the night. Paddy's mind followed the two friends in case Tony should need him. However, the game changed.

The young elf sighed. "Oh, no. I want to sleep."

They flew to the big frozen waterfall, stopped at the top, and slid down, laughing, going faster and faster. When they got to the bottom, the genie took Tony's hand. Suddenly they were on foot, walking behind a curtain of sheer blue ice.

Paddy mumbled in his sleep, "Come on, boys, enough. I want to sleep. Come back." The genie heard him, laughed, but didn't respond.

The cave they were in shone a transparent blue. The genie walked until they found a smaller waterfall with gigantic frozen steps. The game of sliding down went on and on. The strangest thing to Tony was that he was not tired, cold, or sleepy. The little genie took Tony's hand, and the boy was in his bed. Surprised, he looked around. Everybody was asleep, even Dick.

At last I can sleep, thought Paddy.

Tony tossed in his bed and fell asleep. All too soon, morning was showing its gloomy face.

Later Paddy sounded the, "Up, everybody. Time to eat and go."

The weather was not inviting. The gray sky had again a promise of snow.

When breakfast was over, Sabrina said, "It does not seem to be nice out there."

"I know, but we have to move on with the quest, little girl," replied Paddy.

Slowly, they opened the door sighing. Dick rushed out joyously and abruptly stopped, sniffed with his hair up on his back. "I know, Dick. Thanks." Paddy dismissed the house.

"See, we had visitors last night," said Tony to the elf, showing the trampled snow.

"Yes. They were quite a group," he replied, smiling, pleased by the good sense of observation the boy was showing. Almost tiptoeing, they crossed the mesa. The footprints of the goblins were everywhere. The little party, led by Vald, had to descend on the other side of the plateau.

"At least, man, we can see where they are going," said Daryl.

"Providing the wind doesn't come, then the snow will cover their tracks," replied Paddy.

"Never mind, man. Let's move while we can still see where they are going, right?" said Daryl, trying to be cheerful.

The little party had not yet reached the foot of the mountain. Paddy knew that the goblins, traveling on their own ground, would use the best trails. However, it was difficult to follow the group. They were so many that they had packed the snow, making the trail as sheer as a skating rink.

How grateful they were for their elfic boots! The trail led down sharply. Dick had a hard time. Even with his four paws working, he would slide, falling flat on his face, his four paws sprawled on each side of his body like a rug. The children were watching him, giggling.

"I'll carry him," said Vald.

"No, I will provide you with elfic booties, Dick," said Paddy.

"Really? Can you do that?" asked Daryl.

"Of course I can. Just watch."

Paddy moved his hand. The next second Dick was sporting flaming-red boots. They were so light that he didn't even realize he had them on.

"How cute!" said Sabrina.

"Wonderful!" exclaimed Daryl. "Now, my friend, walk properly."

Surprised, the dog took off without any help and looked back at his master, as if to say, "See I can do it."

The children giggled softly.

They reached a sort of gullet between the two mountains, the one they just climbed down and the one they were about to climb up. The weather turned for the worst, with a snowstorm and a terrible howling blizzard.

"If we find a place to stop it will be sheer luck," said Paddy to Daryl walking beside him. The elf's sharp eyes could see the precious goblins' tracks still there to follow. Hoods down over their faces, they trudged in the snow. Vald was glad to be so well dressed. The hood took the shape of his horns and head.

The thick blowing snow made it extremely difficult to see. Paddy worried that perhaps the goblins would sit on the trail waiting for better weather.

Dick was still going with his little elfic boots. The strong wind several times blew the dog away from them. Vald bent down, gently took him in his arms, and put him under his cape. The children gripped onto each other and walked between Paddy and Daryl. Vald was still leading the way. The force of the elements didn't move him. For another half hour they walked painfully in the gully, then Vald came to a halt.

"What is it?" asked Paddy.

"There is a cave on the left," said Vald.

"Okay, I am going to see if it is safe." Paddy cloaked himself. No noise was coming out, so he moved closer to look inside. There was nothing. Arms in the wind, he signaled to his friends to come. When they arrived, he said, "They haven't even stopped. This place was too small for such a large band. We will have to sleep in our capes. There is no place for anything else."

"That's all right, man, providing we have warm food," replied Daryl.

"Just find your place for the night, and we will eat," said Paddy. The young wizard closed the entrance with invisibility spells to keep the wind and the snow out and added a spell of warmth.

Cheerfully, Daryl said, "Okay, man, now we are snug as bugs in a rug. Let's eat. I am famished." A large hot tray with plenty of food landed on Daryl's lap.

Sabrina clapped her hands. "It's like a picnic,"

Dick stayed beside Vald but soon realized that Vald had no people food. He moved over quietly by Tony.

After their meal they rolled in their capes and soon were asleep. The little flickering light appeared.

"Not again," whispered Paddy. He was too tired.

Disappointed, the little light bounced from wall to wall and finally left the cave. Relieved, Tony rolled over and went to sleep.

Chapter 21

Early in the morning a great commotion woke Paddy. A small band of goblins was right in front of the cave. They knew the cave should be there and were frustrated that they couldn't find it. They argued and fought. Fierce blows were exchanged with much screaming.

The young wizard observed the fight and growling.

"This brawl isn't getting you anywhere. Let's move on, guys." Their leader had enough and gave the signal to go. With horrible grunts they left.

Goblins have extremely sharp ears, so Paddy stayed still.

Daryl woke up and whispered, "Wow, man, I am glad you cloaked the cave."

The elf woke the others whispering, "We will take our time to eat. The goblins will be far away when we are finished."

Food at stake, Daryl was all for it. "Good idea, man," he replied.

Paddy added, "We don't know where the big group is, so let's be extremely quiet."

An hour later they left. The snow had stopped, but the wind still blew fiercely. Vald took Dick under his cape. The trail was sheer ice. They progressed, slowly looking for goblins. At a bend of the trail into a huge rock, a large cave was visible. Paddy signaled his friends to halt. The young wizard cloaked himself and crept ahead to check it. About fifty goblins were snoring loudly. Quickly, Paddy cast a strong, long term, sleeping spell upon them and called his friends.

"Here is the large band, sleeping like logs. Let's go."

"Don't you think it's risky to pass in front of the cave?" asked Daryl.

"Oh no!" Paddy laughed. "Not with the spell I've put on them. They are going to sleep for a long time. Not even an earthquake would wake them up." The children giggled.

Vald moved away with Dick safely tucked under his cape. Paddy said to Tony and Sabrina, "Stop, come look at them. I hope you won't ever see their ugly faces again this closely."

Sabrina and Tony approached gingerly. The goblins were wrapped in what was a sort of dark red cape with a brown bonnet where their long pointed ears went through holes. They were sprawled, legs upon each other, with their sharp noses up in the air.

"Wow, ugly things. They stink," said Daryl.

The trail now began to go up the side of the opposite mountain. Once more, they went way up. The howling wind blew heavy clouds of snow at them. Vald stopped and said, "On the other side of this mountain is the lake of fire. The goblins stay there during the winter. Their caves are heated by the fire of the volcano and from the lake."

"Won't it be dangerous to go that way?" asked Daryl.

"I am sure it will be," replied Paddy.

Chapter 22

Elfic biscuits were their ration that day, except for Vald who had his bale of clover. Paddy wanted to be at the summit of the trail before nightfall. They still climbed up for some time. At the top, the trail became narrower. Down in the valley they could now see heavy smoke and steam rising up to the sky.

"The lake of fire," said Vald.

"Wow, how are we going to get by that?" asked Daryl.

"There are two trails. One the goblins always travel on," replied Vald.

"What about the other one?" asked Daryl. Vald had been silent about the second one.

"Difficult, even extremely dangerous," replied the giant.

"Let's hope we won't have to take it," muttered Daryl

"We must sleep here. It's too late now to go farther," announced Paddy.

"But, there is no place," said Tony.

"Look, see that huge ledge up above?"

"Yes, what about it, man?" asked Daryl.

"We are going to sleep there. The goblins will never find us," the young elf chuckled.

"What! It will be impossible for Vald to climb up there," replied Daryl.

"He cannot stay down here," said Sabrina.

"I know. Who said he would?" asked Paddy, smiling at the girl. "Look up."

Vald was already on the ledge with Dick. Sabrina jumped, opened her arms, her doll in her right hand, and flew to Vald, followed by

Tony, Daryl and Paddy.

"Wow! We are a real flying squadron, man," whispered Daryl with a chuckle. Paddy looked at him and laughed. His friend was still the same.

They set foot on the ledge. Paddy said, "We will have a small hut, but you won't be able to stand up, Vald."

"I don't mind," replied the giant.

The young wizard caused a hut to appear with the usual crackling fire in a small fireplace. Vald found himself inside, with the rest of the party. Rustic beds, table, and a bench were the furnishings of the hut.

"How nice to be out of that cold, man." Daryl quickly rubbed his hands by the fire, and Vald said, "Perfect, I even have room to lie down."

"Splendid! I have cloaked the cabin. It's not the time to forget our usual precautions."

Darkness completely covered the mountain, buried under a thick coat of snow. They ate a good supper, then, whispering, sat by the fire. The children played quietly with Dick. Time for bed came. Soon the only sounds heard were the crackling of the fire and Dick snoring.

In the middle of the night, the terrible howling of the goblins filled the air.

Paddy saw the band arriving, snouts up in the air, sniffing and screaming. "Elves! Elves are here!" Their excitement was great.

Paddy whispered to Daryl and Vald, who were now awake, "Don't be afraid. They won't see us. Go back to sleep." After a while the band, frustrated and howling with anger, left.

✳ ✳ ✳

The next morning, breakfast finished, before stepping out they all pulled their hoods over their faces and their capes snug around their bodies. Paddy moved his hand, and when they looked up the ledge was empty above their heads. The snow still came down heavily.

Paddy wanted to be at the lake of fire in the afternoon. On this side of the mountain the path trampled by the goblins had been enlarged and sloped down gently. Heads tucked in their shoulders, braced against the strong wind, they walked briskly. Dick was safely under Vald's cape.

As they approached the lake of fire, the temperature became warmer. Quickly, they removed their hoods. The trail was watery. The snow touching the ground turned to slush immediately. A pleasant summer wind blew.

"Beasts! They have a nice place here, man." growled Daryl.

Vald warned Paddy of caves nearby. This meant the possibility of goblins. The heat as they neared the lake became intense, almost unbearable. The volcano spat fiery lava into the lake. Even from as far as they were, they could hear the water whistling like a kettle.

"Wow!" said Daryl, who compared the sight to a preview of Hell.

"I don't know, I have never been there," replied Vald, candidly.

Daryl chuckled.

"Blast it! A large band of goblins is going across the lake," grumbled Paddy.

"This means we will have to take the bad trail," replied Vald.

"How bad is it?" asked Paddy.

"The trail is unstable. The rocks crumble under foot into the lake. It won't hold me. I will use the goblins' trail and take Dick with me. If he were to fall in there, it would be the end of him. The goblins won't bother me. My size scares them. I will escort you to the trail and go the other way. We will be waiting for you."

They reached the foot of the mountain. Perspiration ran on their faces. Vald showed the way. The trail around the lake had been washed out in many places by lava. They jumped over large crevasses where snowmelt created creeks. In some places the lava was still flowing. It was a game for the children to defy the rushing waters. Paddy's eyes constantly watched them for fear they might trip and fall in the lava.

"Here!" said Vald, showing a rocky passage crossing the lake. "Be careful. I told you, the rocks are cooked by the heat and crumble easily," repeated Vald, worrying for his friends.

Daryl chuckled nervously, saying, "Well, I don't think this is the way to heaven, man."

Vald gave him a quick puzzled look.

Paddy, concerned about the children crossing the lake, made a rapid decision and said to Vald, "I will use my power to send Sabrina and Tony to you."

The giant left with Dick. Tony was bitterly disappointed.

"We have to think of Sabrina's safety, Tony," said Paddy, who knew how much he loved his sister.

"I guess so," replied Tony, downcast.

"Good boy. I will hide you with an invisibility spell, until Vald arrives. Take Sabrina's hand, Tony. Ready?" Paddy moved his arm above their heads and they were gone. "Now I feel more comfortable," said Paddy to Daryl.

"Those children are courageous," replied Daryl.

"Yes, especially Tony." Paddy smiled. "The little girl has her magic doll to calm her. That is why the old wizard gave it to her."

"I was wondering why she clung on to it like that."

"We must go, Daryl."

"I know, man," he replied with a grimace.

"Let's move, then." Paddy slapped Daryl's shoulder. "Just the two of us, like in old times, man."

The young elf showed the way. The lake underneath them was bubbling, spitting lava at their feet. Their elfic boots kept their feet cool. Paddy felt the rocks cracking under his light weight, and he worried because Daryl was much heavier. Paddy asked the human boy to go faster. "Let's walk lighter, Daryl. Put your weight on the balls of your feet."

"You don't ask much, do you, man? I am not an elf you know."

"Yes, but try. Walk ahead of me so I can keep an eye on you."

Daryl, now terrified, replied, "I don't like it. I don't like it, man." He shook his dark hair wildly. They kept their hoods down so the terrible heat wouldn't burn their faces.

"Keep your eyes on the trail. Jump from rock to rock. Don't be afraid man, my wizard's eyes can see through you and ahead of you."

"All right, man. Here I go." As lightly as he could (Daryl had never been a light boy on Earth), he ran on the burning rocks. Paddy was right behind. They had been going for a while when the elf cried, "Watch out!"

With a loud crash, sparks flying all around them, a big chunk of the trail fell into the boiling lava. Daryl couldn't stop himself and teetered over the gap. The young elf grabbed his friend and jumped safely to the other side.

Daryl, shaking, said, "I wish I were an elf, too. Things are so easy for you."

Paddy put him down. "If it's your wish, you can be one too."

Chapter 23

"Really? You bet I wish it!" Paddy smiled, remembering when he was on Earth years ago, how much he too had wanted to be an elf.

"We are not far from shore," said Paddy.

"I am glad, man, I am glad!"

"I see Vald and Dick. The children are with them," announced Paddy.

Daryl jumped faster from rock to rock, happy at the thought of being soon on safer ground and one day being an elf. He made his final jump, greeted by an overjoyed Dick, who had the good sense of not barking. Daryl patted his dog with affection. "Man, I have never been afraid of water, but of that lake, I tell you I was stiff scared."

Sabrina sang and danced. "They made it, they made it!"

Paddy gently said, "Hush, Sabrina! Do you want the band of goblins upon us?"

"Oh, no! I am sorry, Prince Patrick."

The volcano above their heads began spitting fire high up in the air.

Daryl became nervous and said, "We'd better move away. I don't like that. The earth is shaking too much for my own good."

Without waiting for a reply, the human started running on the trail going along the foot of the mountain. Vald followed and soon passed him. Dick, happy to be free, was trotting from one to the other.

Hours later they were still in goblin territory, and night was coming fast. The snow started falling, and the temperature reached an unpleasant coldness. Now, the meager vegetation was covered by a heavy coat of snow, enough to hide from the goblins. They walked in silence.

"Goblins!" shouted Paddy.

"Where? Where?" asked Daryl, terrified.

"Somewhere behind those rocks on the left. I have just been wounded by one of their darts."

"Oh no!" Daryl, Vald, and the children cried in one voice.

"It's bad for us. I am going to lose my power bit by bit. Quick, we must find a place to camp, where I may conjure a strong house. Hurry! Hurry!" said Paddy, running.

They ran as fast as they could, the snow slowing them down.

Vald cried, "Here is a large flat place with high boulders lined up like soldiers."

"Splendid, they will be a good protection for the house," said Paddy. Immediately the elf moved his hands and a large stone house appeared. Quickly, they ran inside. The young wizard could feel his power going, like blood seeping out from his body.

Hurriedly, he cloaked the house with strong invisibility spells and brought lots of food, water, bales of clover, and wood into the house. Then Paddy felt empty. His power had left him. "My power is gone," he said sadly.

A great silence fell upon the house, like when you have lost someone very dear.

"Didn't you say, man, that there was a way to restore it through an old Gremlin's ring?" asked Daryl.

"Yes, I did," replied the elf.

"Then, let's do it, man," said Daryl.

"It's not that easy, Daryl. Tony, and only Tony, can get the ring. Our only consolation is that the goblins don't know the effect of their darts on me."

"That's good, but what do you mean, Tony? I will do it, man," replied Daryl, going to the door, ready to leave.

"You heard me. Only a male elf child can take the ring from the gremlin without dying," said Paddy.

"What!" cried Daryl.

"I will go," said Tony, excited at the prospect of new adventures.

"He can't go alone! He is a child!" said Daryl.

95

"Why not? I am small. I can hide easily, and I have the magic whistle. Beside, you are not that much older than I am." Tony grinned.

"He is right, Daryl, there is no other way," said Paddy.

"But how is he going to know where to go, man?"

"He has the whistle to guide him," said Paddy.

"When do I leave?" asked Tony, anxious to go.

"Tomorrow morning, boy. First, have a good night of sleep," replied Paddy.

The joy they usually shared around the table was missing. Everyone was quiet, lost in their thoughts. The meal over, the little group sat around the fire, with Dick on the floor, his head between his front paws, and his eyes going from one to the other. Nothing was said. After a while, Tony and Sabrina went to bed, followed by Dick, who jumped on Tony's duvet. Soon the young friends did the same.

* * *

The morning was bleak. The sky, heavy with snow, had a sullen look. After a good breakfast, Tony stamped the floor, ready to leave.

"Here, Tony." The elf gave Tony a gold chain that he removed from his neck. "Make sure the whistle hangs under your shirt so you won't lose it. I am sorry I can't do more for you, boy."

"I wish I could come with you, to help, Tony," said Daryl.

"Thank you, I will do fine. Take care of my sister, please."

Tony took his tiny bag with the elfic biscuits and the wonder water, kissed Sabrina and hugged Dick. The dog got up to go with him. "No, boy, you can't come with me, not this time." The dog whined sadly. "Bye for now, Dick, see you soon." He walked out, waving his hand.

Through the window the friends watched the young elf who bravely left alone to get the Magic Ring to restore Paddy's power to continue their quest to destroy Xary.

* * *

Head down, Tony trudged through the snow. The wind was so strong, that he had the unpleasant sensation of not moving. The snow had been falling all the day long, and now it reached almost to his knees. Tony was tired and lonely. Night came, and he looked around for a place to sleep, then he spotted one, in the flank of the mountain, a hole. With a sigh of relief Tony crawled inside and removed the stones from the ground. Satisfied, he sat warmly tucked in his elfic cap, took an elfic biscuit from his tiny bag, and sucked some fresh snow.

Exhausted by the walk in the deep snow, Tony pulled the hood down over his face and fell asleep. In the middle of the night the wee light came and tickled Tony's nose. Half asleep, he mumbled, "Nice to see you. Please, I want to sleep."

The little light giggled and showed the way to the sky. In the dark night large snowflakes were dancing a happy ballet. The genie touched Tony's hand and instantly the boy found himself in a bubble of light, with his friend, chasing snowflakes. They went to the top of the highest mountain. Morning was about to explode in the dark winter sky. By the power of the genie, Tony found himself in his small hole.

A few hours later, Tony woke, ate his biscuit and gulped some fresh snow. Happy, he left, almost bouncing as he walked. His friend the genie had found him. He was not alone anymore!

Tony walked with ardor. It was a clear day. The snow had stopped falling, and the temperature had warmed up. Soon, he would be able to descend into the valley, which already had green grass.

"Hurrah! No more snow!" screamed Tony, joyously skipping.

As Tony came down from the hill, he discovered a small village of very friendly little people. Not dwarves, just tiny people. The children saw him arriving and gathered around the giant, giving him a joyous welcome. Quickly, they took him into the village to the meetinghouse to present their new friend to the chief. Tony crawled on his hands and knees to enter. He remembered Vald and how many times he had to do the same thing. He smiled at the giggling children and sat on the floor. Soon the house was full of wee people. They came in family groups, with lots of noisy little children. The arrival of a visitor seemed to be a reason for celebration. The chief begged the women to hurry and prepare a banquet. It was done in no time. The meal smelled wonderful, and soon Tony had many plates of food in front of him and a whole keg of water. Of course the keg was the size of a large mug.

When the meal was over, they sang and danced around Tony. The children crawled all over the giant boy. Tony's body was a perfect terrain for games. They jumped, hid in his sleeves and pockets, tried to crawl into his boots, but they were magic elfic boots and didn't permit the intrusion. The games went on and on for a long time, with endless giggles. Tony tried to catch them, but they were too fast.

The chief clapped his hands to end the games. "Silence, children, please. Young stranger, would you mind telling us your story?"

"It will be my pleasure, sir,"

Tony started his story from when he and Sabrina left their parents' palace to visit their uncle in the Blue Mountains. When he ended it was morning. Tony couldn't keep his eyes open.

"Thank you for sharing your quest with us. We will talk about it for generations to come. Good night, boy," said the chief. They all left, still talking about the young stranger's story.

Tony was left in the meetinghouse, the only place big enough for him to lie down. Bundled in his cape he slept the better part of the day. No one came to wake him. When he awoke, the happy little people asked him to stay longer. Tony regretfully said, "I would love to, but I can't. My friends are counting on me."

They understood. Friendship, loyalty, and trust were very important to them. With songs and dances, they escorted Tony to the edge of the forest.

The chief's last advice was, "Be very careful, Tony. Don't trust this forest. Bad things happen in there."

"I promise, chief, I will be prudent."

Chapter 24

Tony slowly entered the forest. A strange mist floated around, the ground was so damp that each of his steps made a sucking sound. No birds or any other wildlife was to be seen. The strong feeling of nearby unfriendly presences made him uneasy, and the extreme height of the trees allowed little light to come down, adding to the eeriness of the forest.

Night set in. Tony found a tree with large branches that would offer him protection and comfort.

"I will sleep here," he said to himself. With agility Tony climbed up until he found the perfect branch. Then, with a big sigh, he lay down.

Suddenly, an angry voice asked, "What are you doing? I don't want you here, little vermin." The tree shook violently, throwing Tony to the wet ground.

"What a mean tree!" He walked away rubbing his ribs and slouching.

After looking around for a while he spotted another inviting tree. "Maybe this one will have me. Let's give it a try."

It was a beautiful tree, too. Once more he climbed up and found a good place to sleep.

Then a sharp voice asked, "Who are you? I don't want you in my branches. I am not an inn. Go away, little beggar."

Tony, this time, didn't wait for the tree to shake him off. Hurriedly he flew down.

"Now what? I can't sleep on the ground. It's too risky and wet."

A bit discouraged and tired, Tony searched for a tree where to rest. Then he saw a very, very, tall trunk, old, with no branches at the bottom, only a few in the middle, and some at the top like a large umbrella.

"I don't think this tree will claim that I am damaging its boughs. If I fall from up there, I will be glad I can fly." Tony chuckled. Up, up he went! It was very, very, high. Much higher than any other in the Misty Forest.

"How nice, I am above the mist. I can see the stars in the sky."

Finally, Tony found a splendid soft wide branch. "What a beautiful place to sleep under the stars."

He sat very carefully to not damage the limb. No voice came to tell him to go away. Slowly, he lay down, munched on a biscuit, closed his eyes and went to sleep.

Tony slept well. The sun played on his face waking him up. He stretched his arms and legs, then opened his eyes. Aghast, he looked around. He was on a soft bed in a beautiful room. He hadn't seen anything like it since he left the fairies' palace.

"Where am I?" he whispered.

"In my home," said a voice.

Tony jumped at the sound of the voice, looked around and saw a boy of his size standing at the door. Stupefied, he recognized his friend, the Genie of the Mountains.

"What are you doing here?"

"I told you. This is my place. I live here."

"But, you live in the mountains, don't you?"

"I much prefer the trees."

"How come you are always in the mountains, then?"

"Not always, only when I go to see my parents. I love the trees and the sky."

"I know that." Tony chuckled. "Why did you choose this ugly tree?"

"It's not ugly. It is the most beautiful tree in the forest. I made it appear that way. Like this, no one wants it."

"What do you mean? Who would take it?"

"You know from experience. The mean ones who live on the floor of the Misty Forest, and there are plenty of them. You have talked to some," he said, laughing. "Now get up from that bed. You are rested enough. We will eat and then play."

Tony jumped to his feet. "Yes, I want to eat, but play, no. I don't have time for that."

"We will see," replied the genie.

The table was set with all the good things that Tony loved. When their breakfast was over the little genie said, "Now we are going to avenge your fall from last night."

"I don't want to avenge myself, and anyway how do you know about it?"

"This forest is mine. I know everything that goes on here. Remember, I am a genie. All right. You won't avenge yourself, I will! I don't like to have my friends mistreated. Come and watch."

They left the tree in the gold bubble. Soon they were over the large tree, which had shaken Tony off last night. The genie blew. The wind came up, shaking the tree from side to side. It cracked from the depth of its roots.

A very angry voice cried, "Who is doing that? You will pay for it."

At that moment the tree fell with a terrific crash, followed by a cry of rage.

"Look, look." The little genie plucked Tony's sleeve.

The tree was lying on the ground, roots up in the air. From inside the maze of its roots an ugly little man with a sharp red nose, round face, and black beard, crawled out. Furiously, he pulled at his long dark purple gown, which was caught in the roots. Growling, he ran away.

"He won't come back for a long time!" said the young genie, laughing.

"Yes! But see what you have done. You killed that beautiful tree! It's terrible!"

"Just wait a little longer. We have to make sure the nasty one is gone."

"What do you mean?"

"Patience, Tony." The genie looked afar and said, "Now it's

safe."

The bubble landed. The genie faced the tree and carefully he blew it upright to where it was before. Then with his magic he set its roots back into place.

"There. Now I am going to give it strength. Soon, it will be just like before." The genie cast lots of good spells onto the tree.

"There, it won't suffer at all."

"Wonderful. I am so glad you didn't kill that tree."

"I would never do that! I must leave you now, Tony. Goodbye"

Tony sighed. "Goodbye, and thanks for everything." He turned his back and left, his shoulders suddenly rounded with the responsibility he felt. The genie worriedly watched him go.

The sun no longer shone, and the darkness in the forest was nothing to be cheerful about. The soggy soil was not easy to walk on. Sadly, Tony thought about the sun somewhere above the clouds. He shivered. The forest had changed. The only life form in this gloomy place was some creeping creatures hurriedly going away at his approach.

Hours went by, and Tony wanted to rest. A large decayed tree trunk lying on the ground made a bench for him. A biscuit and a drop of wonder water made his meager meal. He rolled up in his cape, lay on the trunk, and went to sleep.

Terrified, he woke up. He couldn't breathe! He had dreamed that he was bound with ropes! He opened his eyes. It was not a dream! Strong thin threads of white silk really bound him. Several gigantic larvae were oozing toward him. Frantically, he tried to free his hands and grab the whistle hanging around his neck. The monsters bit by bit crept closer. His hands almost numb, in a desperate effort, Tony managed to bring the whistle to his lips. One of the monsters was already crawling on his stomach.

Tony, wishing to be out of the forest, blew the whistle. He found himself in a prairie with a lovely blue sky. Large birds were flying in the brilliant sunshine, which lifted up his soggy spirits and warmed his damp bones. Joyously he walked away, skipping from foot to foot. With his arms spread like a windmill he turned round and round. Sighing he flopped onto the warm grass. Famished, Tony took a biscuit and munched on it. He left, still playing. The birds watched.

In the big silence of the large prairie Tony had the disturbing feeling of staying still. He noticed, far on the horizon, several dark spots. Perhaps trees? He ran to make sure he would be there before dark.

The birds silently hovered above Tony. Still running, he arrived two hours later, and found to his disappointment, only big bushes with branches tightly intertwined. Anxiously, he looked for one with branches reaching to the ground. In a few minutes, he found exactly what he was searching for. A big dome shaped bush offered him an arbor with branches solidly touching the ground. Tony peeked inside. It was a nice place to sleep.

"I don't know if I will be able to crawl in. This bush is particularly thick and tight."

The birds now were lower, closer and bolder. Scared, Tony quickly pulled his hood over his face and forced his entrance through the branches. His Elfic cape was not damaged. Nothing could tear it. When safely inside, Tony looked up. The birds flying low around the bush, screamed and croaked furiously.

"The sorcerer knows I am on my way to the gremlin's cave. He has sent his creatures after me." This was not a comforting thought at all.

Chapter 25

Tony, scared, didn't move for the longest time. The birds, frustrated, left. It became completely dark. The little elf ate a biscuit and drank a drop of Wonder Water. With the hood still over his face, he rolled into his cape and went to sleep.

In the morning Tony looked up at the sky. Nothing was in sight. Carefully he came out. Many heavy black clouds rolled above. The thunder, like an angry beast ready to let go its bile, growled softly in the distance. Quietly the wind came up.

"Bad weather is coming in. I better get going."

Tony ran. The thunder was closer. The soft growling had given place to a furious deafening boom. Lightning split the sky blinding Tony. Rain came down, gently at first, and then suddenly it was a cataract. Quickly, Tony pulled the hood over his face. The wind now howled fearfully around him. It became a hard task for a small elf boy to stay on his feet. Soon, Tony couldn't fight any more. The little elf was tossed like a feather in the terrible gale. He sat with his arms tightly hugging his knees. Even crouched on the ground he was fiercely pushed from side to side. In the midst of this dreadful weather, lonely, almost in tears, a small light came and tickled him.

"Oh! I am so glad to see you. I was feeling abandoned by everybody in this terrible storm."

"I know. Come." The little genie touched Tony's hand. Instantly, he was with his friend in the Golden Bubble, defying the storm, riding the lightning. They played for hours, then Tony found himself in his own bubble having a race with the genie about who was going to get to the lightning first. Then the thunder abated, still growling menacingly in the dark sky.

Tony, came back into the Golden Bubble with his friend, who said, "I will take you to the next valley beyond the hills. You will be able to see the Bald Mountain you seek. It is the old gremlin's dwelling."

"Thank you. I am so anxious to finish the quest. I feel very lonely at times."

The little genie smiled. "I know. Soon you will have what you came for. Be careful, Xary is watching you. He doesn't want Prince Patrick to recover his power. With no power he can't protect Vald."

"How do you know all that?"

"I am a friend of Lord Treo."

"Lord Treo, Master of the Green Forest and Lord of Light?"

"Yes, he sent me to you."

"Wonderful! I don't feel lonely anymore. The Lord gave me a Magic Whistle."

"That is why I didn't help you in the Misty Forest. You have to learn to use your courage, wisdom and decision. I leave you here now. This valley is a good valley. You won't have any problems here."

Tony sighed and courageously walked away.

The country had been washed by the storm, and the earth smelled so good. The leaves shone like jewels. A rabbit, pink nose up in the air, curiously looked at Tony, and hopped around. Tony watched the little fellow for a while and regretfully left.

His eyes followed a wide silvery river going through yellow and green fields.

What a change from the blizzard in the mountain.

His spirits soared with the song of the birds, and he walked briskly for several hours.

Then voices of laughing children reached his sharp ears. Quickly, Tony approached a village. Excited, the children saw him and dashed to meet him. Their long blond hair touched the top of pink, green, and yellow tunics. All wore dark green pants and red boots.

High-spirited boys grabbed Tony's cape, everybody talking at the same time. They pulled him, laughing, to the village. In all that happy noise, Tony understood that he was visiting the Realm of the Elves from the Shining River. Intrigued by the screaming and laughing, the village elders promptly arrived, smiling.

The chief elder came to Tony. "Greetings, young one. What good tidings bring you among us?

"I am Tony, son of King Arz of the fourth Kingdom of the Flying Elves Realm, sir."

"And what causes you, young prince, to be alone this far from your realm?"

"I am on a quest to the gremlin's cave in the Bald Mountain, sir."

"A very dangerous quest, my young prince."

"I know." Tony sighed. "But I don't have any other choice. I must help Prince Patrick, Elf of the First Realm of the Flying Elves, who is on a quest to help his friend Vald, of the Valdos Tribe."

"What's wrong with Vald?"

"Nothing, sir. The sorcerer, Xary, is after Vald to take his magic horns to increase his evil power."

"We know Xary and his evil plots. Thank you, Tony. I won't ask any more questions. Go with the young ones."

Tony's new friends had much to show him. Boys and girls ran joyously to the river. Zyra, the eldest boy, took out from the water a sort of net. Inside, were strange shining fish. Curiously looking at the net, Tony asked, "What kind are they?"

"Don't touch them," said Zyra, "They will burn you. At night they glow like a candle." Giggles from the girls.

Tony looked at the girls. Not understanding the excitement of the young elves for a fish, he politely said, "How nice."

Zyra, with a great smile, said, "Every year we have a festival with music, dance, and good food. But the highlight of the evening is the contest."

Curious, Tony asked, "Contest of what?"

Zyra seriously replied, "Who will have the shiniest fish, and the sportive events."

More giggles from the girls. Baffled, Tony gave them a quick glance and, starting to be interested, asked, "When is your festival?"

"We should have it in two weeks."

"Oh, I will be gone!"

"Perhaps I can talk with the Elders and see if we could have it while you are with us." "Please try. I would like so much to see it!" Now Tony was all excited too.

"Come, then, let's talk to the elders."

Boys and girls ran to the meetinghouse and with much noise bolted inside.

"Oh, slow down, children, what's the matter?" asked the chief elder.

Zyra explained, "We are here, elders to ask a favor for our friend, Prince Tony.

"Which is? Speak, boy."

"Please, would it be possible to have the Shining Fish Festival tomorrow night?" asked Zyra.

"TOMORROW!!" The elder jumped to his feet. "It will be difficult, boys, to organize this big event on such short notice." He rubbed his forehead, thoughtfully. "We will give it thought. Come back later." Dazzled, the chief sat.

The youngsters left, talking, laughing, and slapping each other's backs. In a terrible cacophony, they tried to explain the rules of the contest to their new friend.

Tony laughed heartily, enjoying their enthusiasm. He said, "Please, one at a time. I can't make out anything of what you say!"

They stopped short. The herald was sounding the trumpet to call everyone to the square. The people, curious and excited, arrived. The chief elder stood upon the big rock at the center of the plaza. Clearing his throat, he said, "Friends, after much consideration, the elders are proposing to have the festival of Shining Fish tomorrow night."

"What! Tomorrow!" screamed a woman. "It's impossible!"

"I know. I know it seems to be that way."

"But why, elder?" asked an old elf.

"We have in our midst a young prince on a quest. He is from the Fourth Realm of the Flying Elves. He can't stay more than two days in our village. The boy would dearly love to see our festival."

The talking became as loud as a busy beehive. Then silence fell as a woman stepped out from the crowd and said, "It will be done, elders, for the pleasure of the young boy."

The talking started louder than ever. The chief elder waved his hand for silence and said, "Then, my friends, let's get busy, we have much to do."

Zyra's parents housed Tony and were proud to offer their hospitality to the young traveler. They left to prepare the evening meal.

The villagers, talking and laughing, went their way. Tony followed Zyra's mother to the house, where she served a delicious meal to the family.

When the supper was over, Zyra jumped up from his bench. "Come."

Quickly, they ran to Zyra's room sneaking through the back door. Zyra didn't want his mother to know where he was going. "Look," said Zyra, proudly showing his trophies displayed on a shelf on the wall. Smiling, he showed the trophy he had won the year before. "I had the most beautiful fish, and was the fastest runner without spilling water."

"What do you mean? You have to run with your fish?"

"Yes, and on your head, too." Zyra laughed at the unbelieving look on Tony's face.

"What? On your head! You are kidding."

"No! The fish is in a bowl secured on your head. We have to run, shoot an arrow at a target, and if two contestants have the same score, they fight with a quarterstaff, standing on a log, to determine who's the winner," said Zyra with a chuckle.

"You did all that with the fish on your head?" asked Tony with admiration.

"Yes, I did, and I won," Zyra answered proudly.

"I wish I could participate in the contest," said Tony enviously.

"But you can!" Zyra replied, clapping his hands.

"Really? I don't have a fish, neither a bowl."

"I will get you one, I mean a bowl. The fish you have to catch yourself. That is the rule."

"How do you catch it without being burned?"

"You'll see. Tonight I will show you. Now, let's get you a helmet and a bowl."

The boys were tremendously excited. Everything was a laughing matter, especially when Zyra brought a helmet, which was much too large for Tony. The thing fell down to his nose. Bent over, the boys laughed to tears. A noise in the hall alerted them. Quickly Zyra removed the offensive piece from Tony's head.

It was Zyra's mom. Gently, she knocked and said, "Boys, you should be in bed."

"We will, soon, Mom."

"Good night, boys."

Chapter 26

Darkness cloaked the house. Zyra silently went to the shed and got a small net attached to a long handle, the kind for catching butterflies.

Quietly, he came back and whispered, "Come on, you are going to catch your fish." The boys stepped out in the night.

"Why so much secrecy, Zyra?"

"I don't want my friends, or my parents, to know that you are going to compete with us. It must be a surprise for all."

"Oh, I see! It will be fun," replied Tony, chuckling at the thought.

Zyra took his friend to a spot along the river where hundreds of shining fish were swimming quietly.

"You must enter the water. Your boots will protect you from being burned. Watch the fish, evaluate their speed, then choose a big one and with your net gently catch it."

"That's all?"

"Yes, that's all."

"Sounds simple enough."

Zyra smiled. "Go. I will wait here. Good luck."

Tony, sure of himself, went in the water and watched the fish passing by. Then a beautiful one swam toward him. Gently he put his net into the water and promptly pulled it out. Excited, he cried, "Zyra, I got it! I got it!" He looked into the net. It was empty. "How come? How can it be? I was sure I caught it."

"I know. Patience, Tony, they are very smart. You didn't wait long enough. They see you as much as you see them. Try again."

For hours Tony tried and missed. It was midnight when he got one. Dejected, quietly, he said, "I have one."

"What! You do? You are a champ Tony. I tried for two nights in a row before I trapped one."

"Really?" Tony's voice was more cheerful.

"You bet. It's extremely rare when you succeed the first night."

Tony laughed, feeling better. He had thought he was a misfit of some sort.

"I couldn't give you one of mine. It's against the rules. You have to catch your own."

Silently chuckling, the boys returned to Zyra's home, put the fish in water, and quietly went to bed.

* * *

Next morning the village was in an uproar. The preparations for the evening festivities were going full blast with the ladies talking and laughingly, the children running, and screaming, and the dogs barking. It was a joyous noise all around. Babes and toddlers were screaming for attention. The men brought lots of wood to the foot of the big stone in the plaza. Long tables and benches were set to dine. In a corner a small platform had been erected for the musicians.

At last, night arrived. The villagers arrived in a procession, carrying the food, with sweet beverages. The young folks were not to be seen, as they would appear only at the beginning of the contest, first the girls, then the boys.

Suddenly, the herald's trumpet sounded. The laughter stopped, and one by one the girls arrived, dressed in long white gowns. Their long blond hair shone in the dark, adorned by tiny bottles with little fish inside. They looked like young sylphs. Some had tiaras made of small vessels. Others had them braided in their long golden tresses. Great applause greeted the lovely sight.

Once more the trumpet sounded. The boys marched into the square, dressed in colorful tight pants and white satin tunics. They looked very smart with their silk helmets, the same color as each boy's pants. On the top of the helmet a small basket supported a transparent bowl with a shining fish inside.

Tony, thought, looking at the girls standing in a half moon circle on the small stage, Wow, it's going to be difficult for the jury to decide which one is prettiest.

"Let the games start," shouted the chief elder, raising his hand.

The wizard of the village made the flags fly behind the stage. The trumpet sounded and the games began. Tony had the most marvelous time. The elves cheered each time their guest won. Tony made it to the last game and found that he and Zyra were the finalists.

The boys were to compete face to face on the narrow log with a quarterstaff as weapon, trying to unbalance his opponent. It was a gallant fight. Lots of betting took place. Finally, Zyra threw Tony off the log. Cheers of enthusiasm resounded. Tony, happy for Zyra, shook his hand with energy.

"They were wonderful games, Zyra. Thank you for inviting me to participate."

"I am glad you did. I had a hard competitor to fight." Zyra laughed.

The trump once more resounded.

"Before we eat," said the chief elder, "Let's return our little guests to their home."

Tony, surprised, said, "What does he mean?"

"You'll see. Come, follow the elders."

Softly humming an elfic ballad, they went quietly to the river to empty the contents of the vessels. Boys and girls removed their hairpieces and released the fishes. The water shone brightly.

The elves bowed and the chief elder said, "Thank you, little ones, for the joy you bring to us."

The fish jumped out of the water so high that it was a real fireworks display, and then they swam away. The villagers left the river, singing. Tony was spellbound. He had never seen anything so beautiful as this.

The dinner was delicious. The children ate enough sweets to be sick. All danced to their heart's content. At the end of the evening, the chief elder thanked everyone for helping to make this seasonal event a success. Then he laughed when he said, "Especially in such a short time. Now let's light the fire in thanks for a good year."

A young elf took a torch to the huge pile of wood next to the big stone. It burned high and bright. The heat released by the fire started the fireworks, set by the elders atop the big stone. It was a splendid sight. Each new burst of colors brought screams of joy from the children, who jumped and clapped their hands enthusiastically. Then, it was over. The wood continued burning for a while under the watchful eye of a young elf while everyone went home to sleep.

Tony waited for Zyra who was talking with an elder. Tired, Tony finally went home with the boy's parents and was sound asleep when Zyra returned.

The next morning everybody in the village slept late.

When Tony woke up Zyra was already about in the room putting things away.

"Zyra, when I return home, I will ask the King, my father, to establish a festival like yours. It is wonderful. I will invite you and your family to attend. The only problem is that we don't have shining fish in my father's realm."

"You can find something else. Maybe shining moths or birds," said Zyra.

"Wonderful. We have them. How did you know? I have to go, Zyra. Please thank your parents for their hospitality."

"Just a minute! I am going with you. Let me put my boots on and take my cape and my bag."

"What do you mean coming with me?"

"I will be your squire. I am going with you on your quest to help you."

"But what are your parents going to say?"

"Last night I spoke to the chief elder. He will explain my departure to them. They will understand, and be very proud of me for doing so."

"I am so happy you are coming along, Zyra"

"So am I."

"Then, please give me some paper. I will write a note of thanks to your parents."

Now, everything was in order. The two young elves silently left the little village, en route for Tony's quest. Happy, they laughed in the fresh morning.

"We have to cross the river. Show me where the water is shallow, Zyra."

They raced each other to arrive at the ford.

"Let's go, Zyra." Tony jumped in the water, which barely reached his ankles. He laughed. "We wouldn't drown in here, for sure."

"No." Zyra splashed around like a young puppy.

The boys ran as fast as the wind across the river. On the other side they flopped on the wet sand laughing. Quest, or no quest, for now they were just two young boys.

"I am starved," said Tony.

"Just minute." Zyra took the packsack from his back.

"Wonderful! You brought some food along!" Tony licked his lips.

"It was easy enough with all the leftovers from last night."

"It's surely nicer than elfic biscuits."

"Oh, but I have those too, for later when this food is gone."

"My dear squire," said Tony comically, with his mouth full. "You are a precious thing to have along."

"Thank you, sir," replied Zyra, bowing.

The boys laughed at their little jest. Famished, they ate like two young wolves. When they had finished, Zyra packed his bag and they left running.

The day went fast. They were still in the valley when the sun disappeared over the horizon. The sky grew darker.

"Let's find a shelter for the night, Zyra."

Tony spotted, in the middle of a small forest, a large tree. "Look, that will be perfect. We will be comfortable."

The young elves climbed up. A large branch made a nice place to lie down. The thick foliage was enough to protect them in case of rain. Zyra opened his pack and pulled the food out. Perched on their branch, they laughed a lot as they ate and talked about the Sorcerer. Soon they rolled in their capes and slept.

Suddenly, terrific gusts of wind came up, trying to shake the elves off their branch. The leaves were almost torn off the tree, but the boys were not disturbed in their sleep. The furious sorcerer sent lightning to burn the tree down, with no more success. Then, he threw large pellets of hail to kill them. The pieces of ice slid off the leaves. Hoping to uproot the big tree, the evil one blew even harder, creating a tornado, which promptly died. The tree stood and the sorcerer, growling with anger, threw lightning bolts and left. The boys still slept.

Chapter 27

Tony and Zyra ate a good breakfast and flew down to check out the damage. The grass was all wet and the surrounding bushes smashed and leafless. Their tree was untouched.

"Lord Treo's power has protected our tree from the hail, Zyra."

"Who's Lord Treo?"

"A powerful wizard, Lord and Master of the Green Forest, Seigneur of Light and Peace, and a friend."

"I can see that," replied Zyra with admiration. Each, drawn into his own thoughts, walked silently. The weather was clear.

"Do you think, Tony, Xary had anything to do with the hail?"

"I not only think so, Zyra, I am certain of it."

"He is following you closely then."

"You bet he is. He does not want me to get to the gremlin's cave, but we will."

On this affirmative thought, Tony walked faster. Later on they made a short stop to eat.

"Now down to the basics, the biscuits,"

Tony laughed at Zyra's grimace, thinking about how much Daryl detested them. "It's better than nothing, isn't it?" Tony said with a chuckle.

"I guess so…"

Zyra didn't finish his sentence. A terrifying growl froze their blood. An enormous wild boar was charging full speed at them.

"Up in the trees, Zyra, hurry!" he shouted.

They ran and just had time to climb up. The boar used his head as a battering ram and shook the trunk furiously. His prey had escaped him. For several hours the elves hung on to the branches for dear life.

To their despair the boar would not stop! On the contrary, the beast was feeding his strength on his own fury.

"I don't know for how long I can hang on like this. My arms are getting numb," said Zyra.

"Mine, too. This is not right. A normal boar would have left a long time ago," replied Tony

Suddenly, the tree cracked. Encouraged by the result of its labor, the boar pushed with more ardor. With a tremendous crash the tree fell. Grunting with joy, the monster ran into the branches, ready to tear the boys to pieces.

As the tree fell Tony quickly grabbed Zyra's hand and blew the whistle.

"Where are we?" asked Zyra.

"I don't know."

They were sitting on a large lily pad in the middle of a lake, just as if nothing had happened. The lily pad didn't move, and the boys wanted to reach shore.

"Maybe we should cut its stem," said Zyra.

"I don't think we can. I have the feeling it would be a mistake," replied Tony, soberly.

"Why? We can't stay here forever!"

"Have patience, Zyra. We just arrived."

* * *

Night came. A beautiful moon shone in the velvety sky. Gently, a moon-ray touched the lily pad and, at that instant, it started to twirl and twirl, going faster and faster.

"This not Xary's doing. I can feel it."

"We will soon see."

The lily pad had let go of its stem. Now, they were going up and up till they reached a huge star. Then it stopped in a splendid garden. The flowers were sparkling gems. The sand in the alleys was pure gold, and the leaves on the trees, emeralds, of the most lovely green. In the middle of the garden, a crystal fountain whispered. Uncertain, the young Elves walked over to it.

"It's beautiful," whispered Zyra, very unsure of himself.

No answer came from Tony to reassure the poor, frightened elf. They climbed a flight of onyx stairs. Silently, at the top of the landing a door slid open. They entered into a hall, lighted by crystal chandeliers and another door opened quietly. Tony walked in. Zyra's hand grabbed Tony's doublet.

"Be careful," he whispered in a shaky voice.

At the center of the large golden room, an old personage was seated on a throne of gold encrusted with precious stones. Gentle lights flickered around him. From his whole being a peaceful aura glowed. He looked at the boys with a kind smile. "Greetings, my young friends. I am the Lord of Serenity."

The boys respectfully bowed, then Tony asked, "Why did you bring us here, my lord?"

"You are fighting a dark evil enemy. You, Tony, have received from my old friend, Lord Treo, the protection of a magic whistle. However, Zyra is powerless if separated from you, and is thus in great danger."

"Oh, it's true! I never thought of that. You shouldn't have come with me, Zyra."

The Lord of Serenity smiled. "That is why I brought you here, to give Zyra some power of his own."

"Power for me? But I am a simple folk, your lordship."

The old lord gently replied, "There are no simple people when courage is present."

The Lord of Serenity brought out of his pocket a ring with a pale blue stone. "This is a Magic Ring, Zyra. When you want to receive help look into the stone, think about what you desire, and it will happen. Use the ring righteously, and only in great need. Farewell, boys."

They were now in a forest. If Zyra's ring wasn't there as proof of what happened, the boys would think they had dreamed the whole thing. Tony yawned and rolled in his cape.

"Good night, Zyra."

"Good night, Tony."

* * *

The chattering of a disputing squirrel woke them up. The little guys were having an argument and their tails flailed the air. Tony laughed, watching them. Zyra, chuckling, brought out the elfic biscuits. They sat to eat and talked about the Lord of Serenity and Zyra's ring. When they left, the little chattering friends were still arguing. Tony followed the impulse of the Magic Whistle. Soon they entered into a land of rocky, sandy soil with strange crawling lizards, snakes, and big spiders, inhabitants of this dreadful country.

"I am glad we have our boots. All these creatures are repulsive," said Zyra.

"Not only that, but you can be sure they are venomous, too."

After a long walk, they were tired. It was hot, and the sun's glare blinded them so they didn't see the big hole and fell in, tumbling down. The deeper they went, the larger it became. Tony and Zyra opened their arms to fly and they soon landed in a small cave.

"Now what?" asked Zyra.

"Let's look around and see what we can learn about our prison."

They ran their hands along the smooth walls. Nothing indicated an opening anywhere.

"What are we going to do?," asked Zyra.

"Well, we must find a way to get out of here. I am certain there is one,"

Tony took his whistle and blew. At that instant a door in the wall slid open, showing the entrance of a tunnel.

"Let's go. I have had enough of this rat hole," said Zyra, taking a run for the tunnel.

"No! Don't!" screamed Tony.

Too late. Something pushed Zyra violently on the chest, throwing him to the ground. "What's that?" he said, shaking all over.

"I told you, you should never enter a tunnel without caution. This one is protected by powerful spells."

"How could I know?"

"You'll know now, won't you," Tony chuckled, whispering, "I

will lead the way."

With the help of his power, Tony walked through the invisible barrier. This time Zyra followed prudently. The tunnel was not large. It sloped down and was paved with big rocks here and there making their progress difficult.

"I wonder who put the spells to protect this place?"

The tunnel continued down and then it became flat. Suddenly, it sharply turned to the right. They faced a stone wall. Tony felt the rock face and found a handhold. He tugged and a door opened quietly.

"Surprisingly, the spells were strong enough, but not harmful," said Tony.

"I am glad to hear that," replied Zyra with a grimace.

A narrow flight of stairs carved in the rock climbed up about fifty steps. Tony, leading the way, arrived into a large cave with several tunnels leading out

Chapter 28

"Which one are we going to take?" whispered Zyra.

"Hush, be quiet." Tony stood still. "We take the middle one."

As they moved forward a hammering noise reached their ears. It was coming from the end of the tunnel. They arrived at the entrance of a large cave. Flickering lights and huge shadows projected on the walls terrified them.

"Giants!" whispered Zyra, stunned.

Tony tried to look brave; "I don't think so. It's only shadows enlarged by the light. Be quiet, and we will see who they are."

They walked as silent as mice going to get a piece of cheese on a table, with the cat in the room. At the far end of the cave was a large stone pit with a blazing fire. Five little men were working diligently at melting gold, while two others were pounding hard on the precious hot metal, making thin sheets of gold and laying them flat on a stone table. When cold, three younger workers were carefully rolling them.

"Look at your giants," whispered Tony.

"Dwarves!" said Zyra, surprised.

"Yes. They are real giants at working gold. It's their trade. Later on, their craftsmen will turn the sheets of gold into lovely objects of art. We must not scare them," whispered Tony.

Tony moved forward and was brutally pushed on the chest, falling heavily.

Zyra chuckled softly, "You just received the same medicine as I."

"I guess so. I should have thought about that." Tony rubbed his seat.

"You must use your magic to let us in."

Tony blew his whistle. "Come, we may enter now."

The dwarves had heard Tony fall and looked. Curious and worried, their gentle brown eyes watched the two young elves. With a big grin, Tony introduced himself and Zyra.

Smiles of happiness shone upon the small faces. 'Welcome, Prince Tony," replied the dwarf who seemed to be in charge. "I am Zirug, chief of the workers. If you would please come with me, I will take you to Uriga, our King."

"Thank you, Zirug. We will," replied Tony.

The two young elves followed the dwarf to the back of the cave into a pleasant tunnel with torches secured by large rings in the walls to light the way. They arrived in a hall. Zirug didn't stop there, but continued his way until they reached a carved door and knocked.

A voice said, "Enter."

The dwarf walked into a simply furnished room, with woolen rugs covering the floor for warmth and comfort. On the walls hung long tapestries of vivid colors. An old personage was writing. On his right a gold candelabra was casting a gentle light on the table.
He smiled at the man and asked, "How are you, Zirug? What good tiding bring you to my presence?"

"Your Majesty, it is indeed good tidings. I have the honor of escorting Prince Tony and his squire."

The sharp brown eyes of the old King went to Tony and Zyra. "Who are you? From which realm do you come?"

"I am Prince Tony," replied the teenage elf proudly. "My father is King of the Fourth Realm of the Flying Elves. Zyra is my faithful squire. We are going on a quest to the old gremlin's cave."

"A very dangerous place to go, young ones. Excuse my uncivil way of questioning you, but lately strange things have happened in the kingdom." The King rang for his major-domo. "Artu, we have two noble guests, Prince Tony and his squire Zyra. Please escort them to their chamber to rest."

Artu bowed to the King and to Tony and said, "If you please, sirs, follow me."

Tony, in turn, bowed and left with Zyra. All the way the tunnel walls were handsomely decorated with paintings of flowers, animals and all sorts of vegetation. In places, colorful tapestries hung to the floor. The tunnels, lit by iron torches, had a mysterious look. Above each flame, a hole had been pierced into the rock to let the toxic fumes out. The boys were amazed by this ingenuity.

On their way they met several smiling women with children dressed in brilliant colors. The wee ones giggled at their sight, and were promptly reproved by their mothers.

Artu stopped in front of a door and opened it. "If you please, sirs. A valet will come to help you."

"No need for that, thank you, Artu. I have my squire."

"As you wish, sir. When dinner is ready, a page will come."

The major-domo left. When he was gone Zyra laughed, asking, "Do you always talk that silly way?"

"Yes, of course. It is protocol when I am at my father's court, or in another court."

"It's a little bit stiff, don't you think? I am glad I don't have to talk to you this way."

Tony smiled. "Not now, Zyra, but later on you will. When you are at my father's court."

"Who said I was going?"

"I did. I hope you will, Zyra"

"I don't want to leave my family."

"But they will come with you, silly."

"Ah, maybe then I will come."

The room had thick rugs on the floor and bright tapestries on the walls. The beds were the size of the young elves, as were the two large chairs. Tony yawned, flopped in one of the big chair stretching his legs out. A light knock at the door made him sit up quickly. He said, "Enter."

A small page came in. He was to escort the prince and his squire to the royal table. Quickly, Tony whispered to Zyra, "Now listen, you don't sit at the table. You will stand behind my chair."

"What! But when would I eat then? I am starved!"

Tony, with a chuckle, replied, "With the other squires, when the

King says so."

"Oh, boy! It's terrible! What a horrible thing protocol is. And what if he forgets to tell me to go to eat?" whined Zyra worriedly.

"He won't."

They arrived to the dining room and the little page left. The King had not yet arrived.

Then the herald announced, "Their Majesties, the King and the Queen."

Everybody stood and bowed at their entrance. The Queen, a small lady, gently smiled at the boys. Their Majesties sat at the head of the table, which was in the shape of a horseshoe. Tony was invited to sit by the Queen, and Zyra stood behind Tony's chair.

Then the food was brought. Poor starved Zyra was in agony, but to his joy the King soon asked the squires to leave their stations and go to the table reserved for them, facing the horseshoe. Zyra sighed. He had a hard time to refrain from running.

Tony was asked about his family, his realm and the King, Tony's father. The dinner went on and on. Tony battled bravely to keep his eyes open. The Queen realized what was happening. With a smile she said, "I think, my dear, we should let our young traveler and his squire retire. They have had a long journey."

Grateful, Tony bowed to the Queen. "Thank you, Your Majesty. I accept your kind offer."

He bowed a second time to the King, to the court and, followed by a well fed, tired Zyra, left. The little page was at the door, ready to escort the young guests back to their room. Exhausted, the elves collapsed onto their beds fully clothed, pulled the duvet over themselves, and fell into a deep sleep.

For breakfast the page came several times to rap at the door. It was noon when they finally woke. The page, still waiting, took the young elves to dinner. Their Majesties were not present, only people of the court. Zyra was asked, like the other squires to sit at the table beside Tony. It was a relaxed meal, with loud talking, laughter, and even songs. Elves and dwarves are merry people. The afternoon was well on when they left the table.

A guide was appointed to show the boys the different crafts the dwarves excelled in. Zyra was especially interested in the blacksmith work, and Tony, due to his rank, was attracted by the workmanship of the goldsmiths. The time went quickly.

Once more, the boys were dining at the royal table. Zyra, more relaxed this time, stood behind Tony's chair. Tony asked the King for permission to leave his kingdom the next morning with his squire. Visitors were rare, and they regretted the departure of the elves. Later the boys left their new friends to go to bed. The journey ahead was going to be long.

* * *

The next morning Tony and Zyra were ready to go. After breakfast the major-domo was waiting with a guide to escort the young travelers out of the kingdom. The walk in the tunnels was long, and, without a guide, it would be difficult to find their way out. Arriving at the exit, the dwarf bowed, said farewell, and left.

"How nice it is to see the sky," said Tony.

"But not the wind," Zyra said, shivering, and pulled his cape tightly around him.

The valley below was displaying all the glorious colors of an early fall. From behind a bush rose a large plume of smoke.

"I wonder who's there? I don't see any village," said Tony.

Afraid of unfriendly campers hunting around they moved quietly. The wind, blowing from the mountains they had left, was cold and strong. It howled and shook the trees furiously. Quickly, they put their hoods on. Bent down they walked away. Even for sharp elves ears it was difficult to hear anything except the gale. Suddenly, face to face, they met an Urk coming out from behind a huge tree.

"Run!" cried Tony.

For an instant the startled Urk stood still, then, realizing what he saw, with a terrible roar, like a demon ran after the elves calling, in the same breath, for the rest of the band. Now, the troop was after the boys. The elves were literally flying. Being much heavier, the Urks were losing ground, screaming at the thought of their potential loss.

The boys entered into a thick forest with huge trees. Roots like enormous reptiles crept on the ground, rocks on the pathway slowed their flight. In a mighty leap, Tony was up in the highest tree.

"Hurry, Zyra, climb up. Hurry, they are coming!" screamed Tony.

It was an enormous oak with strong roots anchored into the rugged soil. The large branches with dark green leaves made a perfect camouflage for the two. Shaking, they clambered almost to the top.

The Urks arrived, sniffing the air furiously. Frustrated, they sat grunting, screaming, arguing, and fighting. Luckily for the boys, unlike the goblins, they had a poor sense of smell. Finally, their leader had enough of the brawl. Furious, he pulled ears, administered blows and kicks, and gave the order to depart for camp.

Tony and Zyra, perched on their branch, watched them going away, still rumbling like a storm. "I am glad we had a good breakfast with the dwarves. We better stay here for the night in case they come back, Zyra."

"I agree. The tree is strong and a safe place for us."

The wind had died down. Now that the chase was over, the young friends thought of the noon meal. Out came the elfic biscuits. For Tony they were familiar. In training, at the academy, he had eaten them often. Zyra had not, and even though he said nothing, it was obvious he did not appreciate this kind of meal.

Darkness came. The young elves in their tree, well tucked between branches, rolled into their capes for the night.

"Good night, Zyra."

"'Night, Tony."

Chapter 29

During the night a giant green creature came from underneath the roots of their tree and angrily asked, "Who's on my tree?"

No answer came. Then the boys awoke and looked down at that terrible thing with an enormous round green head and fiery eyes. Huge searching limbs ran through the branches. The creature's arms were so long that he reached the top of the tree with no difficulty. Like terrified squirrels the elves tried to escape the searching arms by jumping from branch to branch.

The growling voice said, "'I know someone is here! Where are you?" The monster continued probing the branches.

That night the elves didn't sleep. As the pale morning light showed on the horizon, the monster, growling with frustration disappeared under the roots of the tree.

"What a night! My legs are worn out by jumping. I don't know if I can walk," said Zyra.

"My shape is as good as yours. I don't want an encore to that performance, doing that silly dance tonight," replied Tony with a grimace. "Let's go. We must leave now." Quickly, Tony flew down.

They looked for an entrance at the base of the tree! Nothing, not even a footprint.

"If it wasn't for my sore legs, I would think I had dreamt the whole thing," said Tony, scratching his head as he walked away.

Thorns and briars were scratching their hands and faces, and they pulled their hoods down. Decayed branches lay on the ground, constantly tripping them. Exhausted, dragging their feet, discouraged, the elves wondered if ever they would come to the end of that nightmarish forest. Still, they didn't dare stop.

"Let's sit down for a while," said Zyra, in a faint voice.

"No way. We can't do that! Do you want to sleep here?"

"Oh, no!" replied Zyra terrified.

"All right, then move!"

With a little more spunk, Zyra marched, munching on an elfic biscuit.

Soon Tony excitedly shouted, "Look! We are out of the forest!"

They ran and collapsed onto a poor ground where meager weeds grew.

Tony nervously said, "I can't believe we are out of that place." Fearfully, he pointed a finger toward the mountains and said, "There is the Bald Mountain where the gremlin lives. We must cross that prairie, then we will be almost there."

The boys rolled in their capes, and lay to rest for a while before starting the long walk across the prairie. The weather was bitterly cold. A few minutes later, Tony got up. "Enough, Zyra, we have a job to do. Prince Patrick, Daryl, and Vald are waiting for our return."

Zyra jumped to his feet. They left, walking briskly. The grass was short so their pace was not slowed, even by the wind. Tony saw a herd of wild horses frolicking in the prairie. Excitedly, he cried, "Look! Look! Let's get some to ride. We will go faster!"

"Are you crazy? I am not a horseman!"

The horses saw the young elves and with a loud whinny from their leader, left in a spectacular gallop.

"Sorry, I forgot you hadn't been brought up to ride. One day I will teach you." Tony sighed. "I wish I were on their backs."

"Not I, thank you! I'd be stiff scared." Zyra laughed.

"I guess you would be!" Tony chuckled.

The prairie was very large. The boys had to face the fact that they would have to sleep in the open. Darkness had come quickly. Too tired and sleepy to go on, they stopped, ate, and without a word, rolled in their capes, pulled the hoods over their faces and immediately fell asleep. It was a cold, clear night.

They had a wonderful rest. Stretching arms and legs they ate a biscuit, drank a drop of wonder water and left. The weather was extremely cold. Zyra rubbed his red nose to warm it up.

Tony, doing the same thing, said, "It's getting colder."

After a long march they arrived at the foot of the mountains, where a game trail led up. Quickly, they began the climb, when suddenly the frozen silence was broken by a furious growl! Terrified they jerked and looked up. On a ledge above their heads was a large bobcat with bared teeth, crouched and ready to spring.

"Run!" cried Tony. They left so fast that the startled cat stopped growling. Then, in a prodigious leap he was after them. Tony yelled, "Zyra use your ring!"

The young elf turned the stone, making his wish. Baffled, he looked at Tony beside him. "How come you are here, too?"

"We had the same idea," replied Tony with a chuckle.

The trail now was much higher. They were at the pass going to the Bald Mountain. The snow was deep, and a large glacier had to be crossed.

"I don't like that," said Zyra."

"Think of it as a game, just like the one at your festival."

"I don't have any other choice."

"Right!"

Gingerly, they walked on the ice. Fortunately, their boots gripped on the slick surface. Nevertheless the boys were very much afraid. Carefully, they moved along the edges of large bottomless crevasses. They stopped petrified. There, in front of them, was a thin ice bridge to be crossed.

Tony said, "Doesn't seem to be very strong. Our best chance is to run."

Frightened they looked at each other and then down. It was so very deep that it was like looking to the bottom of the world! Uncertain they sat for a while.

"We could use our magic," said Zyra.

"No. We are not in peril, yet."

Zyra sighed and with terror looked down.

"It doesn't help to sit here. Follow me and remember, we run."

They mustered all their courage, looked at each other, and off they went. Halfway across, the bridge cracked sinisterly and broke, taking down the screaming boys. Tony flew using his cape. Hurriedly Zyra did the same. All around was beautiful transparent blue ice. Fascinated, the elves forgot their terror admiring that incredible new world. Spellbound, they arrived at the end of their fabulous journey. There, wide tunnels went through the huge blue mountain.

"Which one are we going to take?" whispered Zyra.

"This one. But why are you whispering?" Tony showed a very large tunnel on their left.

"I don't know. Why this one?" Zyra moved away nervously.

"I feel it's the one we must take."

"Okay."

They arrived in a large cave with stalagmites like a gigantic frozen forest. Speechless, the young elves admired this magnificent wonder of their world. Never had they ever seen anything like it. Taken by the magic of the place, they moved silently. Tony took a tunnel on the right sloping up gently, which changed from ice to solid ground. They left the magic cave for rock and earth.

"We are not walking on ice any more," whispered Zyra.

Tony laughed, looking at Zyra, "Why do you whisper? I already asked you that once, I think."

"I guess because of the cave," he replied, embarrassed.

"I understand. It was so beautiful."

The tunnel continued climbing up, the walls bizarrely scarred, chewed. A sweet, fetid smell floated around.

"What's that reek?" Tony made a terrible face.

Zyra laughed. They were not going up any more, the ground was flat. Suddenly, Tony's sharp ears picked up a strange grinding sound coming from afar. "Listen."

"Yes, I hear. What can it be?"

They proceeded cautiously. The tunnel still had small ridges on the walls as if some big claws or teeth had been working there. Just ahead, a big, long, scaly gray creature busied itself chewing at the walls giving morsels of rock to her young who waited between her legs.

"They seem to feed on the rock. Those scratches on the walls are their work," said Tony.

"The question is, are they dangerous?" whispered Zyra. Fascinated by the creatures they were watching, their fear was gone,

"I don't think they even know we are here," said Tony.

"Maybe they don't have any eyes, nose or ears," replied Zyra.

They approached, making absolutely no moves to alert or frighten them, almost gliding on the dust. The creatures peacefully ground their rocks, paying no attention whatsoever to them.

Strange, thought Tony, walking along the opposite wall.

Then, the mother quickly turned around and attacked Zyra. Her huge mouth brutally grabbed the elf, shaking him up in the air. Zyra screamed, which irritated the creature even more.

"Your ring! Use your ring!" cried Tony.

Zyra's trembling hands turned the stone on the ring as he wished to be free, then he found himself with Tony, running, followed by a furious gallop. The tunnel shook under the creature's heavy body. When she judged them far enough from her offspring, she turned around and ran back.

Zyra, trembling, dropped to the ground. Tony sat beside him, whispering. "I really thought she had not seen us. I guess she was watching our moves all the while. Are you okay?"

"Yes, thanks, just shaking a little." Tony helped him up.

"You are courageous, Zyra. I am proud to have you as my squire."

The young elf got red in the face. Bashfully, he replied, "Thank you, Prince Tony."

Tony laughed. "Strong emotions make you very ceremonious, Zyra."

"Just practicing. After all, I must learn to act properly."

"Please, don't overdo it."

"I won't, I promise."

The comrades left and walked for a long time. They reached a natural bridge going over a large underground river. They began to cross it, when in the middle a bolt of lightning hit them. Without the protection of their capes, the young elves would have been killed.

"Someone does not want us here. We must be approaching the old gremlin's lair. Hold onto my hand, we are going through that barrier of spells." Tony blew on his whistle, and they were now sound and safe on the other side of the bridge. "The gremlin probably has lots of tricks up his sleeve," said Tony.

Cats couldn't have walked more silently than they. The tunnel they entered was larger, and well cared for. There were no rocks or anything to make them trip. They moved, tiptoeing, light as feathers.

"We are very close to the old gremlin. I can feel it," whispered Tony.

Chapter 30

Suddenly, while talking, down they went. They had missed seeing a large hole in the center of the tunnel. Now, caught in a net, they hung dangling in front of the cruel eyes of the old gremlin himself. The ugly monster, sitting on a huge throne, laughed. Three of his repulsive minions were at his feet and joined the horrible cackle. The net was drawn so tightly that the elves couldn't even move a hand.

"What a stench in here," whispered Tony. "I can't get my whistle."

"And I, my ring."

"Look! Look! The ring we are after is on his finger. I have to get it," said Tony excitedly.

Then a thundering voice boomed, "Why are you here, elves?"

"We got lost," replied Tony.

"How did you pass through the spells?"

"What spells?" asked Tony, candidly.

"Don't try my patience, elves!" said the gremlin furiously. "You will hang here until you rot."

Lots of gremlins had joined the others in the cave. They laughed and danced under the prisoners and nastily poked the poor helpless boys with long sharp sticks.

"Mean little things," yelled Tony.

The terrible voice of the old gremlin once more said, "Speak! Tell me why you are here. Then, they will leave you alone."

He had a ferocious smile on his large ugly mouth, where long yellow teeth stuck out. His wet, bulging eyes were set on the elves.

"I told you. We got lost," replied Tony.

"Enough! Silence! Do you take me for an imbecile?" roared the old guy. The cave shook. The gremlins stopped their dancing and laughing. The old guy had reached the limit of his patience.

"Get out, all of you! Bring me food!" he screamed. His face turned purple, and his watery bulging eyes literally popped out of their sockets as he shouted. Drool dripped from his terrible mouth.

Quickly, the nasty little crowd left. It didn't take long for food to arrive, carried on the heads of his minions who stood up at the table beside him while he ate. He gorged himself with all sorts of strange, repulsive, smelling things, some still alive and moving on his plate. He ate so much that he fell asleep, snoring. The plates magically walked away and disappeared as quickly as they were finished. No one stayed by his side. The minions left quietly. All alone, the elves in their net dangled in front of him.

"If only we could get free. What a splendid moment to snatch the ring," whispered Tony.

"Yes, but we can't even move a finger."

They had been hanging for a while, like sausages set out to dry in a butcher's shop, when a small light came to tickle Tony's nose.

"What is that?" asked Zyra, scared.

"My friend, the Genie of the Mountains." Tony was so happy to see him.

"Stop it, Iroc. I am going to sneeze and rouse the old guy."

The genie stopped his dance on Tony's nose.

"Please, Iroc, let us out of this horrible net."

Immediately, they slowly fell to the ground.

"Thank you, Iroc," Tony rubbed his hands, shaking himself.

"How are you going to get that ring?" whispered Zyra.

"To my knowledge, there is only one way. Take it off his finger," replied Tony with a grimace.

"You hope to do that?" Zyra, round-eyed, looked at Tony.

"I will try."

The small light, like a busy bee, flew frantically around the gremlin.

"What is he doing?" whispered Zyra, watching.

134

"I don't know!"

Iroc, giggling, said, "I have put a strong sleeping spell on the gremlin. You may take the ring. He won't feel it."

"Are you sure?" asked Tony, touching the limp, pudgy hand.

"Yes, you have my word for it."

Tony, shivering with revulsion, grabbed the cold, slimy hand. Gently, he tried to remove the ring. e whispered, "I can't. It's stuck at the knuckle. He is too fat."

"Now, try again," said Iroc.

Tony took the hand, which was now like jelly, and pulled. The ring came off with no effort at all.

"Thank you, Iroc." Quickly, he put the ring in the pocket of his doublet and muttered, "Let's go! But, which way? We are going to bump into the tribe."

"Come." Iroc waved his hand.

They moved away from the snoring monster and followed the small light. Quickly, they left the cave.

Probably eating, the band was laughing in another cave. Many tunnels were going in all directions. Without hesitation, the light entered a tunnel. Tony's feet barely touched the ground. The elves had been going for a long while when their sharp ears picked up the sound of a riot far behind.

"Oh, oh! The old gremlin has found out why we were in his cave." Tony chuckled.

Iroc went faster. Now the screams were closer. The elves reached the bridge. The small light shone brighter as the genie canceled the spells from the bridge. In one leap they went through. The genie laughed as he put back the nasty spells, but twice as strong as before, and they left.

From far behind came terrible screams. The gremlins were trapped in the genie's snare on the bridge. With no mercy, the spells bombarded them with lightning and serpents of fire. Heartily, Tony laughed, saying, "The gremlins are busy at the bridge. We may slow down, Zyra."

The little light stopped beside the young elves. Tony said, "Thank you, Iroc. I would like to present you, Zyra, my squire."

The genie appeared and emphatically said, "I am Iroc, Genie of The Mountains. I am pleased to meet you, Zyra."

Tony smiled. Zyra, stupefied, looked at the young bald genie, who had a long tress of black hair leaving the top of his head, reaching his thin waist, He was dressed in baggy red pants held at his ankles by bracelets of gold. On his toes shone sparkling rings. An amulet hung on his bare chest.

"I never thought I would meet a real genie one day," said Zyra with a big smile.

"Well, now you have." Iroc chuckled. "I may get you out of these mountains, if you wish. It will take you a long time to return to The Lake of Fire. Remember, Tony, Prince Patrick is waiting for you."

"You are right, Iroc. We can't lose any more time. We accept your offer." Iroc moved away and disappeared.

✻ ✻ ✻

Now, they were in the valley where Tony had met the nice wee people he had told Zyra about. The village was not far. They saw, in the cold air, plumes of smoke coming from the chimneys. The ground was covered with a white coat of snow. Winter had set in.

"It would be nice to stop and see them again," said Tony, "but we are expected by Prince Patrick, his friends, and my sister."

"Your sister? You didn't tell me your sister was with you."

"Sorry, Zyra. We were too busy. I forgot, but you will meet her soon."

Hoods down over their faces, they walked bent against the bitterly cold wind. With a sigh of regret, they walked away from the friendly village. By mid-afternoon the snow had started, and they had been walking in a blizzard for several hours. The deep snow reached almost to their knees. Early darkness had come. They arrived at the place where Tony had slept when he left his friends to go on his quest.

"We must sleep in that small hole, Zyra. I slept there before."

"That's all right, we will be out of the wind."

"We could make a teepee with our capes, but we would be right on the path the goblins use," explained Tony.

"No, thanks. I prefer be cramped up in the hole," replied Zyra.

The boys crawled in, ate their biscuits and went to sleep. The blizzard blew all night.

In the morning the entrance of the hole was completely blocked by the snow.

"I don't think the goblins would have smelled us," said Tony with a chuckle.

With strong kicks the boys pushed through the plug of snow. Bright sunshine greeted them.

"What a beautiful day! I am so happy we got this far. Soon Prince Patrick will have his power back."

Cheerfully stretching his cramped legs, Tony said, "They don't know we are so close. We should be there this afternoon."

Joyously plowing through the snow, not wasting time, they ate while walking, enjoying the sunshine and the feeling of a mission well done.

"Why didn't the genie leave us at your friend's door?"

"I left under my own power. I would hate to come back otherwise. Iroc knew it."

"I see," replied Zyra thoughtfully.

They had been walking for about five hours when Tony jumped with excitement, yelling, "Here we are!"

"Where? I don't see anything."

"Of course you don't. Prince Patrick cloaked the house with invisibility, before he lost his power."

"How do you see it then?"

"Look!" shouted Tony. "It appears and disappears. We have arrived just in time. The spells are fading away."

Tony excitedly ran. He could see Sabrina jumping at the window. From inside Dick barked with gusto.

"It's Tony. It's Tony!" screamed Sabrina.

Chapter 31

Quickly, Paddy opened the door. Dick dashed between his legs like an arrow and jumped at Tony's face and gave him a big smack. Tony fell back on his seat, laughing, with Dick frolicking around him. Promptly, the young wizard pulled him up, pushed the boys inside and locked the door.

Sabrina bolted into Tony's arms and kissed him. "Tony, I missed you!"

"We have a band of Urks looking for us," said Paddy, "and the spells are fading away."

"I know. We could see the house appearing and disappearing," said Tony.

Everybody was staring at Zyra, with curiosity.

"Later I will tell you about Zyra. First, the most urgent thing. I have the ring."

In unison, Paddy, Vald and Daryl said, "Wonderful!"

Soberly, the teenage wizard said, "We must use the ring now. If the Urks were to come by here, they would see the house." He took the ring that Tony held out, then said, "Please move away from me."

They stepped away. The wizard stood alone in the middle of the room. Slowly, he rubbed the stone on his forehead, on the palms of his hands, and quickly smashed it on the floor. The stone shattered into millions of luminous particles, entirely covering the wizard, who vanished in a haze of light for few minutes then reappeared.

Spellbound, his friends had witnessed this fantastic scene. Even Dick was soundless. Paddy smiled. "Here we are. I am myself again, thanks to you, Tony."

"Oh, no, not only myself, Prince Patrick, but my squire, too," replied the young elf.

"Your squire?" asked Paddy as he looked at Zyra.

"Yes, sir," replied Zyra. "I am Prince Tony's squire, by my choice of being so, sir."

"Zyra has the courage of a real knight. We will tell you all about our adventures while eating a good meal. We are starved for real food," laughed Tony.

"Elfic biscuits are wonderful for emergencies, but that's all," said Zyra with a grimace.

"Zyra is not too fond of them." Tony chuckled.

"Ah! Good. A boy after my own heart," replied Daryl, patting Zyra on the back. "How about showing us this marvelous power of yours in action, Paddy, by celebrating with a good large meal."

"I will," replied Paddy, with a laugh. "However, first let me strengthen the spells around the house." Paddy, with his arms widely spread, spun around, mumbling.

"There, now we may enjoy our meal." Paddy brought his hands above the table. The next second it was full of delicious food. Dick barked with excitement.

Daryl laughed. "You too, boy, missed Paddy's good food. We were down to the basics. You arrived just in time, boys."

Vald hadn't yet said a word. He was staring at the two young elves with admiration. Paddy, looking at Vald, said, "Our friend, Vald, is spellbound by the success of your quest. When we have finished our meal, you'd better tell us all about it,"

"We will," replied Tony, with his mouth full.

A terrible bang on the roof made them jump.

"Xary knows you are back. Don't worry. He can't see the house. He is throwing his fury around. It was pure luck that he touched us with that ball of fire. It won't happen again," said Paddy sending a stronger spell on the house.

They sat around the fire. Now, it was time for the boys to tell their story. Dick curled up at Tony's feet and gently started snoring. The boys talked for hours. No one fell asleep, not even Sabrina. They were reliving the quest, good and bad. It was almost daylight when they stopped. Tired, the little party went to sleep. Paddy had provided a comfortable bed for Zyra.

"Good night, Zyra.'

"Good night, Tony."

Only Dick's gentle snoring was heard. The shadows made by the flames danced softly on the walls. The wood in the chimney crackled and sparked. All was quiet outside. Tony's quest was over, but he knew the adventure was not finished.

For the first time the boy slept peacefully. Beside him Zyra was sleeping the slumber of the just. The little party, warm and secure in the sturdy little house dreamed about their future adventures. Outside, the snow quietly covered everything with a white coat. Xary had accomplished nothing and with a display of rage had left.

Paddy and Daryl woke up very late that morning. They looked outside to see the snow still falling.

"I think, man, we had better stay here for the day," whispered Paddy. "Let the kids sleep as long as they want. The boys deserve a good rest."

"I agree it's a very good idea. But please give us something to eat. I am starved."

"That stomach of yours, man, is your master."

"Yup, and a demanding one for sure." Daryl laughed heartily.

A large breakfast appeared on the table. Steaming chocolate accompanied a mound of crescents releasing a delicious aroma. Bacon, eggs, and sausages, were escorted by toast, butter, jam, and honey ready for the taking. The delectable odors woke everybody at once.

Tony, sniffing, jumped up on his bed asking, "What's smelling so good?"

Daryl laughed. "You see, man, I am not the only one. Our little friend loves good things, too."

"Especially after a long diet of elfic biscuits," replied Tony, laughing.

Zyra sniffed the air. "I think I am starved," he said seriously.

Paddy and Daryl laughed. "It's contagious. Better eat."

Dick barked with exuberance.

"Yes, yes. I know, boy, you are like your master!" Daryl patted his dog affectionately.

Vald sat in front of a splendid bowl of fruit, a fresh bale of clover, and a large pail of water.

"It's so nice to have good food," said Tony.

"Yes, we missed it during our quest," added Zyra with a grimace.

"Zyra does not like the biscuits very much," said Tony with a chuckle.

Daryl, stuffing his mouth with a big morsel of ham, replied teasingly,"Well, well, what's the matter with you, boy?"

It was a joyous meal. Happy to be together, Brother and Sister teased each other. The meal over, the teenage friends sat by the fire, enjoying the peaceful moment, while the children played, ran, and jumped on the beds with Dick barking.

The two friends and Vald had stopped talking; the noise had reached its peak. Paddy, chuckling, elbowed Daryl. For sure the boys were letting out their fear and frustration from the past weeks. Then, a great silence set in. Tired and full, they had dropped on their beds. Dick, on Tony's feet, gently snored. Sabrina was whispering to her doll.

The snow outside continued falling. Late afternoon, through the window they saw a band of Urks passing by, bent down against the snow. The leader suddenly looked up in the direction of the house.

"Don't worry man, they can't see us," said Paddy to Daryl, who was fearfully looking outside.

One Urk stopped. Growling terribly, he sniffed the air. The guy following didn't like that, and brutally clobbered him on the head, and to make him move faster, his heavy boot flew into the Urk's posterior. Under the shock, he lost his balance and plunged headfirst into the snow. A formidable fight started, with snow flying all around. The screaming was deafening. Laughing, Paddy, Vald, and Daryl watched, betting on the winner. The leader, furious about the problem, turned back and gave each of the fighters a swift kick in the pants. With no more argument, still growling, they moved on.

141

"Party pooper!" shouted Daryl, forgetting he could be heard by the Urks. "For once we were having fun, and you had to stop the match."

"You are right, man." Paddy laughed. "I really thought the smaller one was going to win. But you shouldn't have cried out like that, man, it was dangerous."

A scream from Tony made them turn around.

"What's the matter, boy?" asked Paddy.

"My whistle. I have lost my whistle!"

With all the noise Zyra woke up, joining Tony in his cries of despair.

"My ring! I have lost my magic ring!"

For a few minutes silence filled the room, then the young wizard spoke. "You haven't lost your ring, or your whistle. It was Borrowed-Magic, to help you both through your quest. Now its over, the wizards have taken them back."

"Oh!" said the boys, disappointedly.

"Don't feel that bad. Everyone has a little magic of his own in his heart," said Paddy.

"I guess you are right, Prince Paddy. I am thankful to the wizard that I had it for a while," said Zyra.

"Me, too. It was great," replied Tony.

"Good, boys. Now, how about having a nice supper?" asked Daryl. "The fight made me hungry."

"What fight?" asked the boys.

"A band of passing Urks gave us a good show," said Daryl, laughing at the memory.

"Oh, we missed it," replied the two young elves disappointedly.

They sat in front of the fire watching the flames dancing joyously. Outside, night had come down.

"Well, too bad, let's eat," said Paddy.

"We must catch up on those meals we have missed." The boys chuckled.

"Yes, and you will be fat, both of you," giggled Sabrina.

"Let's eat," cried Tony, jumping.

Paddy got up, moved his hands above the table. Immediately, delicious food was upon it.

"You must love to eat, man. You bring the most splendid meals," said Daryl.

"Well, not really. This sort of food is always served at the King's table."

"I am glad they do, man. We are eating like kings then." Daryl chuckled.

When the meal was over, they sat by the fire, making plans for the morrow's journey. Sabrina was talking with her doll, and the boys on the other side of the chimney were laughing at some jokes. Dick, much too busy chewing noisily on a large bone, didn't sleep or snore. When came the time to go to bed, to the dog's great disappointment, Daryl took his bone away. "Sorry, boy. We want to sleep, you know."

With a big, "Hmm" and eyes full of reproach, Dick curled up by the fire. Soon, he forgot about the bone, and a soft snore filled the room. It didn't take long for the boys to be asleep, either. Sabrina whispered good night to her doll. Daryl, who had eaten too much, tossed in his bed fighting with nightmares. Finally, he fell on the floor. As he clambered grumpily back in bed, Paddy chuckled.

Xary had not returned. Later in the night Tony felt something tickling his nose. The little friendly light was back, flying around his bed, Zyra's bed, and Sabrina's. Then he sat by Tony's side and whispered, "Come, let's go playing in the snow."

"Oh, no, Iroc, I want to sleep."

Iroc didn't listen and touched Tony's hand. At once the young elf was in the golden bubble, flying through the sky. Big snowflakes danced around them. Suddenly, Tony was in his own bubble, playing hide and seek with Iroc. To his surprise, he realized that he could pass his arms through the magic bubble and catch snowflakes. Quickly he made a big snowball and threw it to Iroc. They had a great time! Their happy laughter filled the night. Then, Tony found himself with Iroc in the golden bubble. "Why did you stop the game?"

"Look. Xary has returned."

"Oh no! If he sees us, he is going to kill us."

"Don't be afraid. He can't touch me. His magic is not strong enough."

At that instant a bolt of lightning shook the bubble. No damage was done.

"See! I told you. He can't hurt us. Let's have some fun."

The bubble, like a huge mosquito, buzzed around Xary. Furious, the sorcerer threw bolts of fire, which boomeranged, shaking him badly. Enraged, he went on and on, until he was completely exhausted. With a loud scream of rage, he left.

Iroc laughed. "It is not today that he is going to bother any of you. He won't have enough power."

Tony returned to his bed. Smiling, he rolled onto his side and went to sleep. In the morning the snow had stopped falling. A deep white coat had covered the mountains and the pass.

"We are finally able to go," said Paddy cheerfully.

"Yes, I will be glad to get away from here, man. We have been cooped up in this house too long."

" Hooray! We are going out. We are going out!" Sabrina danced around the room, followed by Dick barking.

"Yes, we are!" replied Paddy, laughing. "Will you please, stop and come to eat with us before we go."

"Your sister is a lively little thing," said Zyra, smiling at the girl.

To celebrate their departure Paddy brought up a splendid breakfast. Daryl prepared a large bag of leftovers, as did Zyra, not forgetting he was now Tony's squire. The young wizard watched, smiling. They had forgotten that at anytime he could provide food for them.

"Why do you take all that with you, Daryl?" asked Tony.

"What do you mean? Don't you want to eat, boy?"

Tony laughed. " But Prince Paddy may have food for us. You don't need to carry all that with you."

Chapter 32

Poor Daryl's mouth opened wide. He looked like a child caught with his hand in the cookie jar. Paddy restrained his desire to laugh.

"Come, come, Tony! If he wants to do it, that's fine with me. You, too, Zyra."

The young elf was not feeling better, afraid that he had insulted the Prince Wizard. Daryl finally closed his mouth, and said, "All right, I will take this along with me." To reinforce his point Daryl threw the bundle on his shoulder.

Zyra looked at Tony. "I think I will, too, if you don't mind, Prince Tony. After all, I am your squire and I must look after you," he said with a note of pride.

"You are right, Zyra. A good squire must always be ready to succor his prince. The matter is settled. Let's go," said Paddy.

Vald had been quietly observing the youngsters, then he said, "Let's move on."

"We will Vald, we will, indeed," replied Paddy in a cheery voice. "Out, everybody. Out! Or I will take the house from under your feet." With a mischievous grin Paddy lifted his hand.

"Okay, man! Okay." Daryl gave him a bad look and dashed outside. The children ran out and rolled in the deep snow. Dick barked, jumping on top of them. Paddy faced the house and dismissed it whispering, "Thank you for the safety we enjoyed within your walls."

"What's that? Why do you say that, man?"

"Because you always treat good magic with respect."

"Ah." Round-eyed, Daryl looked at Paddy, saying, "Sometimes I think that you are queer, man."

Paddy laughed, and as Daryl turned away, gave him a good kick in the rump jerking the bundle.

Daryl turned around angrily. "Be careful, man, you almost spoiled good food!" Paddy felt his bad mood and didn't answer.

They left, plowing through the deep snow. It was extremely cold but no one complained. They were enjoying the fresh air, just to be outside. The trail was clean with no visible trace of footprints. They didn't take Tony's trail, but instead, turned left between two big mountains.

"Too bad we don't go visiting the little ones," said Tony.

"We are not here for visiting friends, Tony," replied Paddy.

The young elf sighed and said, "I know. I hope one day we will leave behind us all these worrying things."

"We will, boy, we will. Be assured of it," replied Paddy.

Sabrina, her doll crushed against her small chest, looked at the young wizard with fear. She sighed. "Are you sure I will see Mom again, Prince Paddy? I miss her so."

"Certainly, Sabrina, you will. I am sorry the quest takes so long."

The snow was now so deep that Sabrina had a hard time walking. Quietly Vald picked her up and sat her on his shoulder and scooped Dick from the deep snow. The poor dog was fighting valiantly for each step.

"Thank you, Vald. Now I can see very far and poor Dick can breathe too."

"You are taller than all of us," said Zyra with envy.

"Would you like to come up?" asked Vald.

"No, thank you. I will stay with Tony."

In a gully they found a nice place to rest and eat, just beside the trail. Daryl dropped his bundle on the snow, ready to feed everybody.

"Not I, thank you, Daryl. My squire has provided for me!" said Tony.

"Fine with me, boy," replied Daryl.

Proudly, Zyra sat beside Tony, and gave him the food he had brought along.

"Thank you, Zyra. Now take some for yourself," said the young elf.

They were talking joyously when a terrible growl made them jump.

From the end of the gully a fantastic beast charged, a huge lizard with spikes on its back. It spat fire at them. Dick barked furiously.

"Back, boy. Back up!" said Paddy, who tried to stop the monster by sending lightning. Daryl took out his sling and threw a big stone at its left eye and missed. The beast stopped advancing and stood jerking its head up and down and screaming furiously. Paddy fired bolt after bolt at its feet. "Get out of here! Hurry!" said Paddy. "I don't want to destroy the beast. We are intruders and not in immediate danger. We have a way out. Hurry! It's going to charge again."

Vald grabbed Sabrina and Dick. Quickly, they left the gully. The monster angrily spat fire and roared. Paddy gave a quick look behind to see if they were pursued. "We may stop. The beast is not following us."

"What was that, man?" asked Daryl. "Xary's creature?"

"No, only a giant lizard. They are very dangerous when you invade their territory," replied Paddy.

"Wow! I can see that man."

The children were very quiet. They had been really scared.

"The beast must be feasting on our meal," said Daryl sadly.

"Probably." Paddy laughed.

Reproachfully, Daryl looked at him.

"Don't worry, man, you will have a good meal later on. I promise."

Daryl didn't answer, but sighed thinking about the good food left behind.

The danger over, Sabrina asked to walk with Zyra and Tony. The giant let her and Dick down. Zyra, with a grin, brought out from his bag what he had saved from the retreat, and shared it with the two young elves and Dick.

"You are a resourceful squire, Zyra," said Tony. "With you I am sure we won't starve. Thank you."

Sabrina, putting a morsel of bread and meat in her mouth, said, "Zyra is wonderful, Tony. May I have him as a squire, too?"

"No, silly. Girls don't have squires."

"Oh! And why not?"

Her brother shrugged his shoulders with impatience. "Because you are a girl. You can't be a prince. Only princes have squires."

"Ah! Why can't I be a prince?"

"Enough, Sabrina. I told you why. You are a girl," replied Tony, losing patience. The little elf hugged her doll and looked at Zyra sadly.

"I can be your friend, Sabrina," he said with a smile.

Sabrina's eyes lit up. "Really! Will you?"

Zyra soberly replied, "Always, Sabrina."

She sighed. "That is very nice. I will remember it."

When their meal was finished Zyra packed his bag. The two young boys got up and walked away, leaving the girl with Dick, Paddy, Daryl, and Vald. The sun quickly disappeared behind the mountains, night came down.

"Let's find a place where Prince Paddy can put a house," said Tony. "We will go ahead and look."

The trail suddenly became wider. From the left another trail was merging with the one they were traveling on.

"Look, Zyra," observed Tony, "it's all trampled. Lots of people have come this way." They went back to report the bad news.

"That doesn't sound good, man," said Daryl.

"No, probably a band of Urks or goblins!" replied Vald.

They proceeded silently to the merging trails. "Goblins," said Paddy, with a grimace.

"Oh, no! Not again!" cried Tony. "No, this time they won't get me. "

"Then what?" asked Vald, alarmed at the idea of goblins.

"I am going to shroud myself with spells. I should have done it when we left for the quest. It was stupidity on my part to have overlooked such an important thing." The teen wizard made a circle in the snow, and asked his friends to move away. Slowly, he lifted his arms above his head, singing a very soft chant and starting to turn right. A thick mist came up from the ground and entirely covered Paddy.

"Where is he?" asked Sabrina, ready to enter the circle to find Paddy.

"Stay here!" said Tony, grabbing the girl by her sleeve. The others hadn't moved, waiting and watching.

Slowly, the mist vanished. Paddy was still turning, this time to the left with his arms down. Quickly, he erased the circle with his boot and came out. "There, it's done. They can't touch me now."

"For how long?" asked Sabrina.

"Forever, Sabrina."

"Wonderful. Wonderful," she cried, dancing away.

"Hush! Not so loud! Do you want to have the band of goblins coming upon us?" asked Paddy, laughing softly.

"Oh, no!" she whispered, putting her hand on her mouth.

"Cool, man. You are something else," said Daryl, shaking his head in disbelief.

"Good! Now move on." Ready for action, Paddy sure of himself, walked ahead of them.

The trail had become very icy because of the great number of goblins passing through. Hair up on his back, Dick sniffed the ground, rumbling softly.

"Don't bark, boy," said Daryl.

The dog looked up at his master and put his nose back into the snow, continuing his sniffing. They moved quietly, with their elfic ears catching every wee sound.

"They are not far, about a kilometer," said Paddy.

"Wow, man, how can: you tell that?" asked Daryl.

"My ears. Tony and Sabrina can hear them, too," answered Paddy.

"They surely make lots of noise," said Zyra.

"You, too!" asked Daryl.

"Of course. He's an elf," replied Tony proudly.

"I wonder what they are doing," said Paddy.

"I hope, man, there is a way to avoid them," replied Daryl.

"I don't think so," replied Vald.

The trail was definitely larger. A short distance ahead they saw the trail entering a cave and smoke coming out.

"I will go closer, to see what's going on," said Paddy.

Shadow among shadows in the late afternoon, he approached. In a huge cave a large gathering of goblins were around a big fire, feasting, drinking, screaming, and, of course, fighting. The trail was ending there. Paddy returned to his friends with the bad news.

"It must have a way out somewhere in the cave," said Paddy.

"Even if there is one, we can't use it," replied Daryl.

"We will wait. They are doing lots of drinking. Soon they will be in a deep sleep. Then, it won't be too difficult to enter the cave. Let's find a safe place and go to sleep," said Paddy.

"We are all tired. Let's wait until no more noise comes out from the cave," said Daryl, lying down. Everyone wrapped themselves in their capes and did the same.

The young wizard, even in his sleep, could perceive the smallest sound. They slept for many hours. The great noise coming from the cave finally stopped. Paddy silently got up and walked in.

The fire in the cave was burning low, the meager flames giving a poor light. Carefully, the elf walked through the snoring, stinking bunch. About two hundred of them were packed on the top of each other, arms and legs sprawled in every direction. The teenage wizard arrived at the other side of the cave. No one had come to sleep that far from the fire. It was too cold and dark there. The elf's sharp eyes at once spotted the opening of a large tunnel. Paddy went to see if this was another cave. It was not. Quietly, he walked back through the maze of goblins and arrived where his friends slept. Gently, he woke them up.

"There is a tunnel," he whispered.

"Where?" asked Daryl.

"We must pass through the band. The tunnel is at the back of the cave. They are sound asleep. With care we can do it, after I put a deep spell of sleep on them."

"I can't do it, man. You, you see in the dark. For me it will be more than hazardous, it will be deadly! I can't use my elfic stone."

"I know, man. I thought about that. Vald, would you mind carrying Daryl and Dick? You can see in the dark, too.

"Of course I will," said the kind giant.

"Never, man. I am not a babe to be carried in anyone's arms!" said Daryl.

Chapter 33

"Well, then you will have to stay here, waiting for us to finish our quest, with the goblins around. Sorry, man, there is no other way," replied the elf.

"Stay here! Are you crazy?"

"I can't let you go through those goblins by yourself, man. They will get all of us, in spite of the spell I put on them."

"Are you sure, man? I can try. After all, you have put a sleeping spell on them."

"No. It's too risky for our party. If I was alone with you, I would say, let's try, but not with other lives in my care. Sorry, man. I don't want to take any chances, they are too many."

"All right." Daryl sighed.

"Good, man. Now, children, be true elves. No sound, light as a feather, and be very careful."

"We will, don't worry. We are going to be as quiet as pussycats," they said and giggled softly.

"I will carry Sabrina, too," said Vald.

"Thank you, Vald. It will be safer for the girl," replied Paddy.

Vald picked Daryl up like a small child, then Sabrina and Dick. He left silently and went inside. Unfortunately, his large feet became a major problem to find room to step between the goblins. Carefully, he wound his way through, and reaching the other side, gently put down his load.

The teenage wizard and the two young elves struggled through the pack to find their way. Tony passed four of them, tangled in each other. One, from underneath, opened his eyes. The young elf froze with a foot up in the air. He even stopped breathing, not moving an eyelash. The goblin growled and returned to sleep. Slowly, very slowly Tony left. In great silence Zyra followed his prince.

On the other side, Paddy was watching the young adventurers, ready to intervene. He gave them a congratulatory slap on their shoulders, then walked away with Daryl hanging onto his doublet. They were not far enough from the cave to use the elfic stone. A few minutes later, the tunnel took a turn and Paddy said, "You may let go, man, and take your stone out. There is no more danger of being seen by the goblins now."

"At last, I will see where to put my feet. Thank you, Vald, I wouldn't have made it without you," said Daryl.

"I am glad I could help," the giant replied.

The little blue light cheerfully shone in the dark. "Really, it's comforting to look at it," sighed Daryl.

The tunnel was large and rough. Something bothered Dick. The dog stayed close to his master. Great danger was not too far away. Whimpering softly, he looked at Daryl and walked near the little dancing light. "All right, silly. I know you don't like the darkness." Daryl laughed.

For a long time the tunnel was straight and flat, and then it dipped down and began to turn here and there. The cold was great, and they bundled themselves in their capes and put their hoods up. No one talked.

Finally, the silence was broken. "I am starved," said Daryl.

"Me, too," replied Tony.

"Aren't we going to stop to eat?" asked Daryl, becoming alarmed at the thought of no food.

"Yes, yes. We will. Just as soon as I find a comfortable place," replied Paddy.

Soon it began to warm up and they removed their hoods.

"Here we are! This is a nice spot to stop," said the elf.

On their left was a small cave. They entered and sat in anticipation of a delicious meal. The young wizard conjured up a good breakfast. Vald had his usual bale of clover, fruit and lots of water. With his mouth full, Daryl asked. "Where do you think this is going?"

"It has to go to the other side of this mountain," replied Paddy.

"I will be glad when we are outside," said Sabrina, "I hate tunnels. I like to see the sky."

"So do I," replied Daryl.

"If you have finished, let's go. You want to be out fast. All right, let's not be sitting and talking," said Paddy.

The elf got up. The children jumped onto their feet and followed.

"Come, Daryl," said Sabrina. "Hurry."

Dick was still waiting for his master and the little blue light. Vald, enjoying his fruit, finished it slowly. He knew that in two steps he would catch up with his friends.

"Are you coming, Vald?" asked Daryl.

"Yes, I am," he replied, still eating.

"I am waiting for you."

"No, no. I will catch up with you."

"All right, hurry then. You shouldn't stay here by yourself!" Daryl left, followed by Dick, who was whimpering. Worried, the dog looked behind. Daryl's logic was telling him that he shouldn't leave the giant alone. It was very dangerous. But, on the other hand, he didn't want to hurt his feelings.

"Where is Vald?" asked Paddy.

"Finishing his fruit. He didn't want me to wait for him."

"It's foolish!" replied the young elf.

"I think so, too, but he is stubborn."

Vald was just getting up, when a terrible growl made him jump in terror! Trembling, he looked around. A monster with two heads was coming at him. The beast spat a slimy liquid, which burned the giant's fur.

Paddy heard the growling.

"Vald! He is in danger," said Daryl.

Paddy left, running. When he arrived his heart sank. Poor Vald was lying on the ground all burned, moaning and trying to protect his face. His body was covered by the thick, white, slimy liquid. The young wizard became furious and fired lightning at the monster. The beast's left head turned its anger toward Paddy. It opened its huge mouth and threw a jet of liquid at the elf. Before the lethal thing had time to reach Paddy, the wizard burned it in midair and with a powerful bolt of fire destroyed the monster, reducing it into cinders.

Paddy and Daryl went to their wounded friend. The poor giant was curled upon himself. Without a word, Paddy lifted his hands above the giant's head and softly whispered some magic words. Like a very fine snow, a shining powder fell upon Vald.

Daryl, Tony, Zyra, and Sabrina had watched the terrible battle. Dick was trembling beside his master.

"This is why you stayed with me, boy. You knew all along the beast was there," said Daryl to Dick, patting his head. "Next time, my friend, I will listen to you."

Bit by bit, the soft shining snow disappeared. Vald's beautiful white fur was restored. Still shaky, the giant got up.

"How do you feel, Vald?" asked Paddy.

"Fine, I guess. Thanks to you, Prince Paddy."

"We must stay together. It's much too dangerous to be apart. That was another of Xary's creatures. The problem is that we don't know when he is going to strike next," said Paddy.

Vald was heavyhearted that he hadn't listened to his friend Daryl, and by not doing so he had endangered Paddy's life by bringing upon the elf this terrible battle.

The young human felt his remorse, and said to him. "You know, Vald, even if you had been with us, this would have happened anyway. The beast had been following us for a long time. Dick knew it, and I ignored his warning and called the poor dog, silly, when it was I, who was silly."

"Thank you, Daryl. I guess both of us are at fault," replied Vald.

Daryl gave the giant a friendly slap and walked away with Dick. After the terrible cold they had endured, the temperature had become pleasant. With a sigh of relief they rolled their capes and stored them in their bags. The tunnel, now very large, had strange plants growing along the walls.

"See! See! We are outside! There is the light!" cried Sabrina.

"I don't think so. I know how much you would like to be out, but this is not the end." replied Paddy.

They couldn't see the source of the light. Surprised, they arrived in a beautiful park. Flowers and trees were growing there, and all around were shrubs in bloom. Under foot, in the alley was a fine sand. They walked silently for a long time. Then, the sound of rushing waters reached their ears. Behind a bush appeared a very high waterfall. Down below the water swirled and boiled, releasing a large plume of white steam, which gave humidity and warmth to the flowers and trees in the park.

"How can this be? Under the mountains!" asked Daryl.

"I think we are going to know that, soon," replied Paddy.

A shining amber light approached them, stopped at Daryl, and curiously went around him. Then, it went on to Paddy, the children, and Vald.

"Welcome to my realm," said a soft voice. A beautiful young woman stood before them. Her shining, silvery hair touched the ground. She had a strange smile on her pixie face and in her large aquamarine eyes burned a cold light. She wore a white floating dress, as light as the steam rising from the river. The garment was held at the shoulders by a gold buckle and bracelets of the same precious metal closed the ample sleeves at her wrists. Around her small waist, a belt of gold had long tassels brushing her tiny crystal slippers. On her right hand sparkled the most extraordinary ring with a huge stone, exactly the color of her eyes.

"I am Sophra, Fairy of the Steaming Waters."

"I am Prince..."

"I know who you are," she interrupted abruptly.

Daryl looked at Paddy.

"You will find all the fruits you desire. Enjoy the garden. I will come back."

She disappeared just as she had come.

"Pretty impolite, that lady," said Daryl.

"I am afraid you are right, man," replied Paddy.

"What does that mean, I will come back? Does she think we are going to stay here forever?" asked Daryl.

Paddy didn't answer. His mind was too busy reading the fairy's thoughts. The young wizard finally said, "Yes, it's what I thought. We are her prisoners."

"Prisoners!" screamed Daryl.

Chapter 34

"Let's find a place where I can study her intentions, without her knowledge," replied Paddy.

Quietly, they left the waterfall going deeper into the garden. They found some big rocks where they sat. Paddy looked in the direction of the waterfall and closed his eyes. His face turned pale, almost transparent, and his eyes rolled under his eyelids in a fast motion, then stopped. "Yes! Yes," he said, opening his eyes.

"What is it?" asked Vald and Daryl at the same time.

"All right! Now I know how to destroy the spells she put on us when she turned slowly around us."

"Spells! What spells, man! She put spells on us?" screamed Daryl, horrified at the thought.

"Yes, I felt it, but I had to be sure."

"Nasty little woman," shouted Daryl.

"She is not little, and she is not what she appears to be. What you see is a deception," said Paddy.

"How are we going to get free?" asked Vald

"Did you notice the large ring on her right hand?"

"Yes, but what about it, man?" asked Daryl.

"I have to destroy it."

"What! How do you think you are going to do that?" asked Daryl.

"I don't know yet, but I will. I have to find out exactly where she lives, or better yet, wait for her to come back."

"Does she know you are a wizard?" asked Vald.

"No. When she was turning around Daryl, I shielded myself."

"I don't trust the fruits she has in her garden," said Tony.

"Eat only the ones I take for myself. Providing food for us would give me away."

"Then I will be an exotic bird feeding on fruits! Nasty, nasty woman!" said Daryl with a grimace.

"Why can't you give us food now? She can't see us," said Sabrina.

"Oh, yes, she can, " replied Paddy, smiling at Sabrina.

So they walked peacefully through the garden, eating the same fruit that Paddy ate. Once fed and tired by their long walk in the tunnel, they rolled in their capes and slept under a large tree. Paddy's mind watched as he slept. The fairy silently approached the little party and went to Vald. She looked very closely at his horns and touched them lightly. Paddy, in his mind's eye, saw a smile of triumph on her thin lips. All her sweet beauty had disappeared. Her eyes were cold as ice and her mouth cruel.

The elf continued observing her. She glanced at him, completely unconcerned, and went to Daryl. Puzzled, she stayed for a while in front of the human, glanced at the children, and went away.

✻ ✻ ✻

When they woke up, Paddy, smiling, said, "We had the visit of the fairy during our sleep."

"What did she want?" asked Daryl.

"I didn't ask. She was very busy looking at Vald's horns."

"Oh, no," said the poor giant, terrified.

"Like Xary, my dear Vald, she is after your magic horns. I am certain that I must destroy her ring. That is our best chance to escape."

"Maybe she is here listening to your plans, man," said Daryl.

"Perhaps, but she won't understand what we are saying. It will be only small talk to her."

"Nevertheless, I am scared," said Vald gloomily. "Now, I have two after me." He looked around. His large gentle brown eyes rolled in his frightened face. Vald sighed.

They walked in the garden, eating fruit, and approached an enormous weeping willow with long supple branches, gently swaying.

"What a beautiful tree!" said Daryl.

"Don't move any closer," screamed Paddy, jumping to pull him back.

Too late. The long branches, like tentacles, flew out and bound all of them. Shrill laughter filled the park.

"Now what?" asked Zyra, bound so tightly that he couldn't move a finger.

"All of you be still. She will come to see why we don't fight the branches," whispered Paddy.

"And what then?" asked Daryl. "I don't want to see her face again."

"Hush, man, remember, this is the only way I can get at her," Paddy replied softly. "Quiet, here she comes."

The fairy was no longer the beautiful young woman, but a very old bony one, with a cruel smile. In her eyes burned a strange light. The ring on her finger flashed. "Well, well! My job is going to be very easy," she said, laughing loudly.

She walked by Paddy, past Daryl. Ignoring the children, she went straight to Vald. "At last, I have you," she said to the giant. "Xary wants you, too, but I got you first!" She cackled and again laughed loudly. Very slowly, she approached Vald. "You know what I want, don't you, large one?" She smiled cruelly at him.

Paddy quietly freed his right hand from the grip of the vine and watched the fairy. She was not in a hurry to get what she desired. Sophra was stupidly savoring her victory over Xary.

That was a big mistake!

The ring on her right hand threw huge sparks and broke in a thousand pieces leaving her powerless. A scream of rage filled the park.

"Who did that?" As she yelled, she turned around to see.

When the ring broke, the tree let go its prisoners. Terribly frightened, Paddy's friends came beside him.

"Don't be afraid, she can't do anything to us now," said Paddy.

She screamed, "You are the one! How come I didn't feel you were a wizard?" Her thin lips foamed with rage.

The elf smiled, "I shielded myself from you."

With the little bit of power she had left, the witch (because she was one) shrieked and vanished into a dark cloud of smoke.

"We had better not stay here any longer, man. This may have alerted Xary," said Daryl.

"Yes," replied Vald, moving away, anxious to get away.

All danger gone for the time being, they left with Dick trotting happily beside the giant. Their prime worry now was to find a way out. After a long walk they were suddenly faced with a very high wall of granite, as slick as ice.

"Wow. Where to now, man?" asked Daryl.

Paddy walked along the wall checking every crack with his powerful wizard's eyes. "Ah! Here it is," he said.

"What? What do you see, man?" asked Daryl, looking at where Paddy was staring.

"Here, do you see these engravings?"

"Nope, just small scratches in the stone."

"They are runes. Runes engraved by dwarves," replied Paddy.

"Fine, but what are they for and what do they say?" asked Daryl.

"I can read runes," said Tony.

"Wonderful.'" Paddy smiled. "Tell us what you read."

Proudly, the young elf approached the wall. "It's a little bit too high for me to read. Will you please hold me up Vald?"

"Certainly."

Vald held Tony at the level of the runes. The young elf tried to understand and couldn't. "It's strange. I can't make head or tail of it!" he said.

"Not so, Tony," replied Paddy. "They are magic runes. That is why you can't read them."

The wizard came closer to the wall and some runes began to glow. With the shining ones, Paddy made words, and repeated them three times. Slowly, the stone wall moved showing a passageway into the mountain. Cautiously, they walked in. When the last of them had entered, the door silently closed. The large tunnel had a floor of fine sand. For Daryl it was very dark, so he took his elfic stone out.

"Look, iron torches on the walls," said Tony.

"Yes, this is the workmanship of dwarves," replied Paddy.

"Good. We are going to meet them," said Sabrina. "I love dwarves. They are nice."

"Perhaps!" said Paddy softly, staring far down the tunnel with worried eyes.

"What's bothering you, man?" asked Daryl.

"I don't know yet. Things in my mind are not quite the way I would like to feel them."

"Another fairy?" asked Vald, eyes full of fear.

"No, something else."

Daryl looked down at Dick. He was acting normally, playing with Tony. This time he was not going to ignore his warning. They traveled for several hours, meeting no one, passing through cave after cave, some beautifully carved. But no sign of dwarves.

Daryl, surprised, said, "The place seems to be deserted."

"Yes, man, that is my feeling, too. Emptiness filled by fire," replied Paddy.

Dick's hair was now up on his back, and he growled. "What's wrong, boy?" asked Daryl, attentive to Dick's reaction. Just ahead was the opening of a large cave.

"Stay here," said Paddy, "I am going to see what's upsetting Dick so much. I, too, feel a great danger."

Light as a feather the elf walked to the cave. Cloaked by the darkness, Paddy stopped at the entrance and, with a start, backed up. On the far left side, two huge dragons were watching two young ones playing in the middle of the cave. Paddy quietly came back.

"A family of dragons occupies the Dwarve's Realm. That is why they left," Paddy whispered.

"How many?" asked Tony.

"Two adults, with two young ones."

"Wow! How are we going to deal with them, man?" asked Daryl.

"We'll see," replied Paddy. "First things first. Tony and Sabrina, you are going to fly as high as you can to the other side of the cave where the tunnel is. Stay and hide there until we arrive."

"I can go across, too," said Vald, with a trembling voice. "By pointing my horns at them they won't see me."

"Wonderful. Then you carry Daryl, Zyra, and Dick. Myself, I have work to do. I am going to try to get those monsters out of the Dwarve's Realm."

"How are you going to do that, sir?" asked Zyra.

"I will. Now do what I said, go."

The children, flying silently, went up, and up, avoiding being seen by the baby dragons playing below. Quietly they landed, sound and safe, on the other side, and hid in the tunnel.

Trembling, Vald took Daryl, Zyra, and Dick in his arms and slowly entered the cave. Head down, horns pointed, Vald faced the dragons. The teen wizard, ready to succor him, watched each of his moves. The children were holding their breath. At last, the giant arrived.

Paddy moved his hands, then gently pushed the young dragons back to their parents. The dragons saw the intruder, and furiously they blew fire at him. Calmly, the elf covered the roaring, fire-breathing family with a heavy mist, snuffing down the flames they were blowing. Paddy looked up at the roof of the cave and turned very fast with his arms stretched above his head. The cave glowed, trembled, the roof cracked, and with a terrible noise, tons of rocks fell like a huge hailstorm inside. Neither the dragons nor the wizard were hurt. Paddy had protected them with strong spells. In a formidable explosion the top of the mountain flew up into the air, revealing the stars. As they saw the sky, the dragons roared furiously. The male flew away, followed by the young ones and the female.

With bolts of lightning the young wizard burned down the debris from the dragons and cleaned up the cave thoroughly. His friends rushed to Paddy and praised him. Embarrassed, he said, "Truly, I didn't know I could do it! I simply tried. My power is increasing, I guess. A few months ago I wouldn't have been strong enough to accomplish such a thing! Uncle Niko would be pleased."

"I am glad you could," said Vald.

"Now, the dwarves are going to come back into their realm," said Sabrina, jumping with joy.

Tony, being practical, said, "It would have taken ages for them to clear up that mess, and the smell!" He wrinkled his nose with disgust.

Paddy replied, "Yes, the air is fresh. Now, guys, all of you move away, and I will close up the roof."

They went back into the tunnel and watched. Paddy began whispering and turning very slowly. His arms were horizontally extended. He brought them quickly up above his head. At that instant, the mountain shook with a terrible noise, and the cave was dark. Each piece of rock was perfectly in place. With a sweeping gesture, the wizard removed the dust and gravel from the ground.

"There,'" he said with a smile of satisfaction.

Chapter 35

Curiously the children looked around the cave.

"See! those nice stone benches along the walls," said Sabrina.

"I am going to sit on this lovely one," said Tony.

The boy ran to sit down. A large horse head carved on the armrest caught his attention, and he touched it. Silently, the wall behind him opened, revealing the entrance to a smaller cave.

"Look! Look, Prince Paddy, the wall is open," said Zyra excitedly.

Daryl, followed by Dick, was ready to enter. Paddy stopped them, "Is there any danger in there, man?"

"It seems that I will never learn. Okay, man, sorry."

"Don't apologize. You have learned so much since we left. Now let me see if there is.

The young human's eyes shone with excitement. "Really, man?"

"Certainly! Now, please, let me see."

The elf went into the cave. It had tables and benches of stone like a dining room, but no rugs on the floor, or tapestries on the walls, so dear to the dwarves. "It's all right. You may come in."

"Oh, it's nice! See the lovely carvings on that wall," said Sabrina.

"Why don't we eat here? After all it's a dining room," said Daryl. "I am starved! Living on fruits hasn't filled me up, man! Plus all the excitement! I am overdue for a good meal!"

Paddy laughed. "Even fear does not cut your appetite!

Daryl laughed. "Nope!"

"I am starved, too," said Tony.

"Me, too," replied Zyra. "

"Me, too! Me, too!" sang Sabrina, laughing.

"All right, all right! You're going to eat. Sit down at the tables. You will be served," said Paddy, cheerfully.

A splendid meal was served. Even Dick sat on the bench beside his master, waiting for his share of the banquet. All the excitement had made a hole in his stomach. For him, too, eating fruit was not his forte.

"Wow, man, it's good, very good!" said the gourmand, Daryl.

They enjoyed that quiet moment.

✳ ✳ ✳

The day was at an end, so Paddy proposed to spend the night here. All agreed, and used the stone benches as beds. Paddy provided some nice feather mattresses. Yawning, they rolled into their capes and went to sleep. Vald, on the floor, stretched himself onto a large straw bed. Dick enviously looked at it and decided to sleep with him. His master's bed was so narrow! He would be much safer with Vald. It didn't take long before Dick's soft snoring filled the small cave.

A small light danced around, then stopped on Tony's head, tickling his ear. The little light giggled and continued until the boy opened his tired eyes.

"Hi! Iroc!" said Tony, half-asleep. "I am glad to see you, but I am terribly tired." Tony turned on his side and went back to sleep.

Iroc was there to have fun with his friend, not to watch him sleep. So he tickled him some more.

"Please, Iroc, let me sleep."

"Come, Tony. I promise you won't be tired after."

Tony, against his wish was in the golden bubble. They flew fast, very fast in the tunnels.

"I am going to show you something, Tony."

"What?" asked Tony, grumpily.

"You'll see, it's fun."

"Sure?" asked Tony, still unhappy.

They arrived in a small damp cave, with a large hole in the center of the floor, and one above into the roof. Tony could see the sky. The heat was great, and the ground around all wet. From below the

166

surface of the hole the sound of rushing, whistling water reached Tony's ears. The earth shook! Then, a huge jet of boiling water rushed out from the hole in the ground. Iroc, in the golden bubble, jumped onto it. With a tremendous force the boys were projected outside. They went high, high in the sky. The jet stood up into the air for the longest time. At first, Tony was petrified with fear, then at the top of the jet, he laughed and danced with Iroc in the golden bubble. As fast as it had come up, it went back down into the bowels of the earth. They played for hours, going up and down with the steaming geyser.

When the game was over, Tony found himself on his soft mattress. He rolled in his cape, smiling, and fell asleep right away.

Daryl was soon up and about, claiming he was starved. Dick agreed with his master, and barked loudly.

"Why all the commotion?" asked Paddy, rubbing his eyes.

"We want to eat, Dick and I," replied Daryl, laughing.

"Goodness, man! All that noise, just for food," said Paddy with a chuckle.

"Yes, man, my stomach is empty, and wants its due."

"Sincerely, Daryl, I wonder how come you don't get sick by eating so much?"

"Force of habit, man. Force of habit." He laughed.

On the table appeared a large breakfast.

"Wow, that's what I call a breakfast," said Daryl as he licked his lips.

Wakened by the delicious smell of hot chocolate, the children opened their eyes. Their noses were at table level. They turned on the bench at once and put their feet under the table and sat. Everybody ate.

When the meal was over, Paddy left the table to look around for an exit. He searched, with no results. "It can't be. There is a door somewhere," the elf said to himself.

"Problems, man?"

"Yes. It seems there is no door. I know there are several tunnels behind those walls. I can blast a hole, but I don't like that. I will, as a last resource."

"Well, let's look, then," said Zyra.

He jumped to his feet and started to search like a hound dog. Tony and Dick followed. Everybody was on the hunting path. At first, the game was fun and the children laughed a lot, but after one hour they all became discouraged and sat down. Only Dick continued patiently sniffing around every inch of the room. Then his tail wagged, and he barked.

"Did you find something, boy?" asked Tony, going to see.

The dog was still barking. Tony didn't see anything. "You are a silly dog!" he said to Dick.

"Don't call him that, boy. The last time I did, it almost cost Vald's life," said Daryl.

"Let's see," replied Paddy, going to look to see what was exciting Dick so much.

At first he didn't notice anything, then, exactly where Dick was sniffing, was a small rock in the shape of a thumb sticking up out of the floor. Paddy pressed on it, and a door silently opened.

"Good boy! Good boy," he said to Dick, patting his head gently. "You see, Tony, you must never take lightly a dog's warning," Paddy said.

"I am sorry I called you silly, Dick," said Tony.

"All right, all right. We have lost enough time, let's go," said Vald, patting Dick.

"You are much more clever than we are boy," said Zyra to the dog.

Paddy went through the door with the children and Vald.

Daryl quietly said to his dog, "I am so proud of you, boy. You are a great help on our quest!"

"It must have been a special place, for them to have hidden that room," said Vald.

"Yes. I suppose," replied Paddy.

The tunnel was large with lovely carvings on the walls. Iron rings hung empty of their torches.

"The dwarves have left their realm. But for where?" asked Tony.

"You can't blame them, what with having dragons as tenants," said Daryl.

Soon, the tunnel branched into many, and they realized that this was where the main part of the dwarves had lived. They continued in the main tunnel and arrived at the center of the city. The dwellings were empty, and only a few stone benches were in the halls.

"I must find where they are and tell them their realm is safe now," said Paddy.

"How can you do that?" asked Sabrina who was always very interested in the dwarves.

"I will use my wizard's power to search for their sage's mind. Then I will communicate with him, Sabrina."

"Wonderful," said Sabrina, jumping happily,

"We will stay here, in this dwelling. Please don't talk. It would disturb me."

The teen wizard sat on a small bench and covered his face with his hood and like a statue stayed still. Several hours went by. His friends were sound asleep. The silence was complete, even Dick didn't snore. Paddy sighed and pulled the hood back. His eyes were still full of mystery. Dick woke up and came to him.

"There, boy, I found them."

Chapter 36

"You did!" cried Sabrina, waking up.

"Yes, I did," Paddy replied.

Sabrina jumped with excitement. "When are they coming back?"

"The King will be here tomorrow. He has asked us to stay at the palace until he arrives."

Daryl had wakened and was following the conversation. "This is marvelous, man."

"Where is the palace?" asked Tony, now awake, too.

"The King, through his sage, gave me the directions."

They left the dwelling and walked for a while in halls and tunnels to arrive at the Palace. It was built in terraces in a huge cave. Beautiful balconies, carved in the rock, faced the large plaza below. Graceful stairs had handsome iron banisters elegantly going up. All the apartments opened onto balconies.

They went up and up, with Paddy leading the group to the throne chamber, up to the last terrace. It must have been beautiful, when lived in. Rich rings of gold hung on the walls, and heavy gold ornaments were still there. A fresco of splendid sculpture ran around the walls, and the place where the throne had been was still visible. Silently, they visited the deserted palace.

They walked down to the terrace below. There, they found a lovely apartment, daintily decorated with flowers and birds in pastel colors.

"Let's stay here, please," said Sabrina. "I love this room."

"Fine with me," said Daryl.

It was late, and after a small meal, they went to sleep. They enjoyed a very peaceful night. In the morning, excited at the thought of meeting the King, they didn't spend much time eating. Even Daryl didn't complain. Dick rushed to the door.

Paddy said, "Our little friend has heard our visitors climbing up the stairs." The elf went outside on the balcony to meet the dwarves.

"Greetings, and welcome to our kingdom restored to us by your hands, Prince Paddy. I am Jorga, King of the Dwarves of the Geyser Mountain."

In the kind face of the old man shone gentle blue eyes. His long white beard touched his rich garments. A red coat embroidered with gold was clasped with a large diamond. Fine brown leather boots, with gold buckles, reached his knees. A huge diamond embedded in a ring of emeralds hung on a heavy chain of gold on his chest.

A handsomely dressed young man escorted the King on his right and on his left an elderly one. The King said, "My son, Prince Murga and my Prime Minister, Lord Ruga."

The teenage Prince-Wizard felt a little uneasy in the presence of these two ancient ones. Courteously, Paddy bowed, introducing his friends. "Prince Tony and Princess Sabrina, from the Fourth Realm of the Flying Elves. Vald from the Valdos Tribe. My dear friend Daryl, a mortal from the Earth Realm, and his brave dog, Dick."

"Welcome to all of your friends. My people will be back this afternoon. Since your communication with our Sage, everyone has been busy packing. After the dragon's invasion, we moved not too far from here. It is a smaller mountain, and we were really crowded there, especially for the little ones. It was difficult for them to play. We are so thankful to be able to return," said the King.

"But the dragons may return," said Tony.

"Yes, my young prince. I have sent men to close the cave by which they entered, and since yesterday they are working at it."

Paddy said, "Please escort me there. I will close it in a second."

"Wow, man, can you do that?" Daryl looked at Paddy with awe.

"Really?" asked the King.

"Yes. The same way that I forced the dragons out." To the King he added, "It will take time for your men to make it safe. The dragons may return any time."

"Thank you, prince. Let's go, please, before my people arrive with the children."

The King showed the way. They walked a long time to reach the site where the crew was working diligently. The men had little to show for all their hard work. It was a big task and would have been so for anybody, except for a wizard, or an earthquake.

Paddy turned to the King, and asked him to call his men inside. "'Please, Your Majesty, tell them to stay well back from the entrance."

The King went outside to his men. "Prince Paddy, a powerful young wizard from the elves' realm will help us close the cave entrance. Please move away and come inside."

One hundred men came in and two hundred eyes anxiously looked at the wizard who was almost a child! The King and escort breathlessly watched the young wizard.

Paddy bowed and moved away from the crowd and his friends. "Daryl, keep Dick safe."

Paddy closed his eyes, slowly stretched his arms in front of him, and whispered magic words. The dwarves stopped breathing, but nothing happened!

Then, out of the teen wizard's hands, came bolts of fire crashing on the mountain. Tons of rocks fell in front of the opening. The job was almost finished when the dragons appeared, trying to reclaim the entrance by blowing tremendous jets of fire into the cave. The dwarves screamed in terror. Paddy threw powerful spells to shield them from the flames. The hole was way too small for the dragons to enter. Their furor was great, and they roared in rage as an unconcerned Paddy continued closing the mountain! Now, he could barely see them, then the hole was shut.

A formidable, "Hurrah,'" filled the cave, rolling down the tunnels.

The dwarves danced, jumping like children at play, and joyously slapped each other on the back.

Tony, Sabrina, Daryl and Zyra were saying, "Cool, cool, man. You did it!"

"Yes, I did it, didn't I!" Paddy laughed, proud of his accomplishment.

Suddenly a great silence fell. Quietly the dwarves gathered around Paddy and respectfully touched his coat.

Bonnets crushed in their hands, they humbly said, "Thanks." Then, as the realization of what had been done sank in their exuberance overcame them. They realized that without Paddy all of them would be dead by now.

Paddy, embarrassed by all the fuss, grabbed a young dwarf by the hand, laughed and said, "Let's go home

"Wow! This is indeed a magical world. I love it, man!"

The happy crew left running, singing, dancing, and shouting at each other.

"We owe you so much, my young friend," said the King, beaming from ear to ear.

"I am glad I could help. I was here at the right time," replied Paddy.

The families who had now arrived joyously greeted the working crew, and everybody went about the business of settling into their former homes. Great festivities went on, and on, for days. The happy people didn't know what to do, to thank the young wizard.

* * *

After five days the party left their new friends. Everyone was there to say goodbye. Music, songs and laughter escorted them. Their sojourn underground had been so long, that once outside the mountain, they found it wonderful to breath the fresh air. They stopped and looked around.

Down in the valley, they could see that spring had arrived, but in the mountains, winter was still in control. Joyously, they took the trail leading down.

Dick barked, jumping around, inviting Tony, Zyra, and Sabrina to run.

"No, no, boy, it's better if we stay close together," said Paddy. Disappointed the dog looked at him. Paddy laughed.

"When we are down in the valley, you will run, but not now. There are still Urks in the mountains."

The mild temperature, the warm sun, the birds singing in the bushes made everyone feel wonderful. Soon, they found shrubs with small green leaves.

"See, see," cried Sabrina, "Leaves, green leaves."

They were so anxious to be in the valley that they forgot to eat. Even Daryl had ignored his growling stomach. The sun was setting when they reached a grove of pines at the foot of the mountains.

"We will stay here for the night," said Paddy.

"Splendid, man. I am starved. We will finally eat," replied Daryl.

"Yes, I am starving, too," said Paddy, with a chuckle.

Daryl found the perfect spot, a beautiful large pine to sit under. Expectantly they waited for the promised food. It arrived! A l-a-r-g-e meal!

Dick's anxious little nose was up in the air sniffing with delight. He sat beside his master, waiting patiently for a morsel. Daryl had always been generous. The children ate silently. Everyone was tired by all the walking they had done that day. The meal over, they rolled in their capes, and in the night full of spring perfume, they went to sleep.

A sunbeam brushed Paddy's face. Smiling, he thought, How nice to hear the voices of birds in the trees.

A big gray squirrel sat on its tail, and boldly looked at the elf, asking, "What are you doing here? This is my realm."

Paddy laughed.

"Well! We have a visitor. Welcome little fellow," said Daryl.

"Right now he is unhappy. We have invaded his realm and he wonders what we are doing here," said Paddy.

"Just passing through, little friend, just passing through," replied Daryl who daringly bolted after the squirrel to catch it.

"Be careful, man, they have sharp teeth." Paddy chuckled.

The boys opened their eyes. Zyra said, "Oh, see, Tony, a squirrel. I am so happy. It seems I haven't seen one for ages."

"Yes, our sojourn in the bowels of the mountains was too long," replied Paddy.

"How nice, we have the visit of a forest host," said Vald.

"You better wake up your sister, Tony. Breakfast is coming right now," said Paddy.

Tony shook Sabrina like a rag doll. "Wake up. Hurry, we want to eat and go. Or do you prefer to stay here by yourself with your doll? You have the choice, you know."

The girl opened her eyes at once. "Stay here alone, are you crazy? Never!"

"Well, then, get up!"

Chapter 37

The breakfast was joyous. Dick barked as he ran after the squirrels, having the greatest time of his life! So had the chattering, teasing squirrels. The forest, warmed by the bright sun, released the sweet smell of pine. For two hours they walked in the shade. It was pure delight. Watching the little rabbits going about unafraid was a joy for all. Even Dick, chasing after them, was taken as a game by the little hosts of the forest. The squirrels chastised him, but after all, that was what squirrels did.

As they followed the well-marked trail, they saw in the distance, between huge trees and bushes, a rock formation with a waterfall splashing into a large pond. The sunshine through the branches was playing on the silvery mist, and a rainbow ran from the mist and disappeared at the top of trees. They stopped, entranced by the enchanting vision of a white unicorn drinking quietly from the pool. When Paddy moved, she lifted her head and ran to him. The friends froze. She gently touched the young wizard with her golden horn, and immediately he found himself upon her back, flying high into the rainbow.

"What's the meaning of this? Where is she taking Paddy?" asked Daryl, completely astonished.

* * *

The young wizard didn't feel any hostility from the unicorn. After a while riding the rainbow, they arrived in a place that was the exact replica of the one they just left. At the edge of the pool lay the unmoving body of another, smaller, unicorn. Paddy jumped down and walked to the unicorn. He noticed that she had been fighting and was badly wounded.

Speaking mind to mind, the young elf asked, "What happened?"

"We were attacked by Xary, the sorcerer. Because of you he has not been able to get Vald's magic horns, so he tried to get ours, which are more powerful. My younger sister has been badly hurt. I managed to chase Xary away. I knew where to find you, so I brought you here to help. Xary will come back to finish her off."

"First, let's heal your sister." Paddy removed his cape and gently put it on the wounded Unicorn. A gold mist covered the small body and a few minutes later she was standing.

Mind to mind, the young unicorn said, "Thank you, Prince Wizard."

Suddenly the ground shook, and Xary in all his horror appeared, throwing bolts of fire at the two unicorns. Paddy quickly moved his arms, shielding the sisters. Xary became enraged and turned his fury on Paddy. It was a fierce battle. The forest around became red. Finally, Paddy threw a huge ball of fiery thread, which bound Xary in its web. On fire and howling in pain, he left.

"There, I don't think he will bother you any more,"

The unicorn touched Paddy with her golden horn, and he was once again on her back, riding the rainbow, followed by the younger unicorn. His worried friends were waiting for him.

"Goodbye, fair ones. Read the signs and take care."

The unicorns bowed twice and whinnied joyously as they left in the rainbow.

✳ ✳ ✳

"What happened man? Where did you go?"

"I will tell you all about it, as we walk."

So, while walking, Paddy animatedly recounted the battle with Xary. He finished his tale just as they entered a large fertile valley. The orchards were in bloom, looking like big bouquets of flowers on the green carpet of the fields.

"Wow! What a lovely sight," said Daryl.

"I don't think we could see anything prettier," replied Zyra.

"Oh yes! In my realm, the Promised Valley," said the teen wizard, proudly.

"Really? It seems impossible," said Tony.

Sabrina was admiring the lovely view. For the little flying elf, who lived in the royal palace at the top of a splendid tree, this was quite a sight! Their realm, of course, was beautiful, too. But this!

"Let's meet the people, who are taking such good care of this valley," said Paddy, walking on.

Their surprise was great. Not a man or woman was in sight in the fields, only a boy who fled as they neared. It was mid-afternoon, after a long walk, before they arrived at the nearest village.

"Strange, man," said Daryl. "You would think this place would be bursting with laughter and song. But no, only silence, everywhere."

"This troubles me deeply," replied Paddy. "I sense something very wrong."

The village had been abandoned! The village's inn was completely silent.

"Where is everybody?" asked Zyra.

"That's a good question," replied Daryl.

"We will stay at the Inn for the night, and see what tomorrow brings," said Paddy.

The innkeeper being away, the young wizard provided food for them. It was a cool night. Daryl lit the wood in the chimney. Quietly, they rolled in their capes by the fire, and went to sleep.

In the middle of the night, Paddy became aware of something coming, something evil! Tiptoing, he went to the window. The full moon was bright, and the square fully visible. What he saw almost terrified him. This was what had caused the villagers to move away.

Ten horsemen, draped in red, hoods down to hide their faces, were mounted on beasts, which emitted terrible growls, with fire coming out of their nostrils. Huge yellow fangs stuck out of their drooling mouths. They formed a circle and started to go round and round in the center of the square. Daryl, Vald, and the children had awakened and joined Paddy at the window.

"What's that man?" whispered Daryl.

"Demons from the Dark Side."

"How come they are here?" asked Zyra frightened.

"I have the suspicion that Xary has called upon them," whispered Paddy.

"But why?" Tony asked.

"He knows that we are getting too close for his own comfort. I am afraid the demons are going to feel our presence," whispered Paddy.

The elf just barely finished saying that, when the Evil Ones turned their heads toward the inn.

"Here, they are coming," said Paddy, shielding everyone with strong spells, including Dick, who had jumped into Vald's arms.

As if on command, the demons lifted their heads and screams filled the village. Their fiery eyes turned toward the travelers, the Evil Ones charged toward the inn.

The wizard and his friends, quiet as mice, retreated by a small back door. The screaming bunch rode into the house, searching in vain. Enraged, they rode out and set fire to the little Inn. The demons stayed around until only a pile of ashes was left on the ground. With a final loud howl they departed. Paddy waited for a while and with a sweep of his hand restored the inn. "We must leave. Staying only makes matters worse for the villagers."

"But what of the people?" asked Zyra. "They have lost their village. How can they come back?"

"That is my problem, Zyra," replied Paddy.

Daryl called attention to a barn in a nearby field. "Let's go there to sleep," he said.

"Good idea, man," replied Paddy.

Blending in with the shadows of the trees and houses, they quietly left the restored Inn for the barn, a comfortable old building with lots of hay.

"The Evil Ones probably won't be back tonight. We may sleep in peace," said Paddy.

They rolled in their capes and went to sleep. Dick, still scared, curled up by Vald's side. His soft snoring was not to be heard that night.

179

* * *

The morning was beautiful. In the bushes the birds were singing, greeting the brilliant sunshine.

"I am going to visit the village," said Paddy.

"I'll come with you, man," replied Daryl.

"Okay. Vald, please stay here to protect the children."

The two young friends left the barn, followed by Dick who walked warily, nose to the ground, busily sniffing. They checked the stables and barns. No animals had been left behind. Cats and dogs were gone, too. The village was completely deserted.

"Poor people," said Daryl.

"Yes. Xary is very desperate to have been calling upon the Dark Side for help. He knows how dangerous this can be. He will have to pay dearly for that call."

"What are you going to do?"

"We are in the square, right?"

"Yes, so what?"

"I think that every night they come here for their merry-go-round. I am going to put spells into the circle." Paddy laughed. "I tell you, man, tonight you are going to see a terrifying show, the best you have ever seen." Paddy chuckled. "Stay out of the square."

The young wizard followed the trail marked in the square by the Evil Ones. Arms stretched in front of him, whispering, he drew symbols in the air and retraced his steps, changing symbols six times around. "There! We may join the others now," he said satisfied, with his work.

"Wow. What a great performance! But, if they come back while we are away, we will miss the show!"

"Oh no, they are creatures of night and never come during the day. Don't worry, we will be here when they return."

"How will you know, man?'

"I will, don't worry man, I will." Paddy, jumping joyously, said. "I will race you back to the barn." They dashed to the old barn.

Dick was still behind.

180

"Come boy," Daryl called. Hair up on his back,

Dick was busy sniffing the circle Paddy had made. The boys stopped running

"Dick does not like your handiwork, man."

"I can't blame him," said the elf, laughing.

"But, if Dick can smell your tricks, so will the Evil Ones."

"They won't. Dick is pure of heart, they aren't. That is the difference."

Daryl looked at his dog, puzzled by all this magic wizardry. "I see," he whispered, not certain that he saw anything at all! Dick, on the contrary, seemed to be completely at ease. Daryl shrugged his shoulders. "Oh, well, I am not going to worry about it. After all, this is another realm." He walked a little bit faster.

Paddy, smiled. He had followed Daryl's thoughts.

In the barn their friends waited anxiously. Paddy cheerfully explained what he had done. "We must stay here, inside. I will know when they are coming," said Paddy.

"Oh. What a pity. It's so nice out," said Sabrina.

"We don't want Xary to know that we are still alive, do we?" asked Paddy.

"Of course not," she whispered, cuddling her doll.

Zyra gave her big smile. "You are a very brave princess, Sabrina." She smiled back. "Thank you, Zyra."

Then, Daryl came up with his favorite, "Let's eat! I am starved." All laughed.

"Yes, good idea, man. That will occupy our time. We will have a large meal. How about that?' asked Paddy.

"Cool, super!" exclaimed Daryl, clapping his hands vigorously, his mouth all set for good food.

The human teenager in all his mortal life never had such a meal. The children giggled, watching him to put away all this food. Rounded eyes they wondered how large his stomach was. And when was he going to stop? Sleepy, the young folks, gorged with goodies, lay down in the hay. Dick loudly snored at Tony's feet. Daryl finally quit, and instantly fell asleep. Vald, sober in all matters, had gone to sleep a long time before.

Night came. In the silence, Paddy waited. He felt the Evil Ones approaching. Gently, he shook Daryl. "They are coming, man. Hush, no noise. Only the two of us will go. Okay?"

Chapter 38

"Like in the old times on earth, man." Daryl replied softly.

"Yes. Come on." They found the proper place to hide near the square.

"I am going to shield us so they won't feel our presence." Paddy had just finished putting the spells upon them, when the band of evil ones showed up on the path leading to the square.

Immediately, on entering the square, the leader circled around followed by the others. They went faster and faster. Up, and up they flew into the air, screaming, burning, and crackling like fireworks in July. The smell was repulsive. The circle of fire turned until only ashes were left on the ground.

"Wow, man, you are something else!" said Daryl, aghast.

"It's over. The village is free." Paddy jumped and clapped his hands in glee at the thought of how Xary must be taking this. Daryl joined him, dancing on the ashes.

"Xary will not call upon the Dark Side twice. It will cost him too much!"

Their dance finished, Paddy, with a sweep of his hand cleaned up the ashes. Silently, they returned to the barn. Daryl flopped on the hay and had a hard time going to sleep. He tossed and tossed. He was finally realizing the formidable power his friend possessed. This troubled him! In his mind he saw the shy little boy, Paddy, on Earth. He had always been afraid and now, in this realm, he was a powerful young wizard! How strange and wonderful! He sighed, and at last fell asleep.

* * *

The morning sun woke the young boys, ready for action.

"Let's go to see what's going on at the village," said Tony.

"But, if the Evil Ones are there," said Zyra, a little scared.

"No way. Prince Paddy said they don't show up during the day. Come, brave squire," replied Tony with a chuckle.

Free as young colts, long blond hair floating in the wind, they left running in the sunshine. They arrived at the square. Nothing testified to the destruction of the evil ones. The boys sat on a bench, legs dangling, watching the water in the small fountain flowing out, murmuring softly. The birds had returned, bathing joyously.

"How nice, the birds are back to sing in the trees. What happened?" asked Zyra.

"Paddy has something to do with that," replied Tony.

"You mean, Prince Paddy?"

"Of course, not me, silly." Tony laughed.

Chuckling, Zyra imagined Tony doing some wizardry tricks. Daryl and his friends arrived, followed by a bouncing Dick.

"Look, Prince Paddy. The water is flowing and the birds are back in the trees, too!" said Zyra.

"Good! That means things are back to normal now."

"There, see! The villagers are coming back, Sabrina," said her brother.

"Yes, they are," said Vald.

A long line of elves, with carts pulled by animals, entered the square. Paddy went to meet them. The teenager said, "Welcome to your village. How did you learn that you could safely come back?"

"Greetings, strangers. I am Turas, chief elder. This morning, the birds in the forest sang, giving us the news that all was well, that we could come back to our homes. The Evil Ones were gone," replied the ancient one

"We were almost killed by their evil doings," replied Paddy.

"How did you escape?"

"I destroyed them all. I am Prince Patrick from the Promised Valley, a young wizard in my own right. I would like you to meet my friends, Prince Tony, Princess Sabrina, Zyra, Daryl, Vald and Dick."

"Will you be our guests, please, and honor us with your presence?" asked the elder.

"Thank you very much, Turas, but we can't. Xary is getting too bold. He must be stopped soon."

"If you are on your way to restore peace and happiness to our country, young ones, I won't insist."

"Farewell, Turas. Prosperity to your village," said Paddy.

The elves cheered their liberators, who in turn waved, goodbye.

The sun shone brightly. They had once more won a battle over Xary and they were happy. Dick enjoyed himself running with the boys and barking at every bird flying by. Sabrina explained, to her doll, Amie, all about the wild flowers and the singing birds. The little elf had a lovely time. Meanwhile, the young men were talking with animation about the quest, trying to figure out how close Xary's lair was. They traveled for days in the peaceful valley, here and there meeting elves who were tending their flocks or their fields.

"It seems Xary has forgotten all about us," said Daryl.

"Don't believe it, man. He is probably preparing one of his tricks, lulling us to feel secure so he can strike."

"Do you think so?" asked Vald, looking around suspiciously.

"Oh, yes I do! He will attack."

"Well, man, at least we have a little bit of peace, to enjoy this beautiful valley," replied Daryl optimistically.

Vald, as if to discourage them, said, "Soon, we will entered the Hills of Mystery."

"Why, that name?" asked Zyra.

"Because many who have attempted to travel there have never returned to tell us about them," replied Paddy.

"Not very encouraging, man," said Daryl with a grimace.

"It can't be worse than what we have been through already," Paddy replied with a chuckle.

"I guess you are right, man."

The evening was a little bit chilly, and they looked for a place to set camp.

"Look, here is a nice grove," said Daryl.

Luscious grass beckoned them. Sighing, they flopped heavily at the foot of a clump of birch trees. In a few minutes, Paddy had food for them. The long walk had given them an appetite, and they ate with ardor. Tony and Zyra watched Daryl put away a terrific amount of food, even more than usual. The human looked back at the boys with a large smile. Dick, sitting beside his master, was gorging himself, too. The meal over, hoods drawn over their faces, all went to sleep. Dick crawled under Vald's cape, and soon he gently snored.

In the velvety sky, full of sparkling stars, the moon shone in all its glory. Something very large moved toward the sleeping group. A green cloud crawled over the ground and covered the sleepers, trying in vain, to burn through the capes.

Early in the morning, Paddy felt that something evil had happened during the night. Through his hood he saw a wet green slime covering everything around, including them. "Poison!" he whispered. His friends were waking up. Hurriedly, he cried, "Don't move! Stay still! Vald, keep Dick covered"

"What's the matter? What's that green stuff, man?" asked Daryl.

"Poison," replied Paddy.

"Poison! From where?" asked Tony.

"Xary. Now stay still. I am going to get rid of it."

Paddy made small signs with his hand. A light smoke rose from the ground and each cape, as the poison burned away. "You come out only when I say so. Okay?"

The elf caused a strong wind to remove the poisonous fumes from the grove. Half an hour later, the air was pure.

"Okay, come out now. The immediate danger is gone."

Dick had had enough of being cooped up under Vald's cape. He rushed out, barking and jumped on Tony and Zyra, who had just gotten up. Dick wanted to play, and he wanted company.

"All right, boy, we are coming," said Tony, and he and Zyra started running and laughing. Life was good on such a beautiful morning.

"Stay around. You don't know what's waiting for you out there," said Paddy.

186

"We will." Tony laughed.

Running and laughing the boys threw a piece of wood to Dick who promptly brought it back. To their horror the wood got bigger and bigger and changed into a slithering, bouncing, monster, a scaly serpent with huge fangs, ready to swallow the boys. Screaming with terror, with Dick's belly almost touching the ground, they ran back to camp, followed by the hissing beast.

Daryl took his slingshot out, yelling to Paddy, "Paddy! A monster! A monster is after the boys!"

Dick, shaking his fear, turned around and jumped on a loop, biting furiously at the beast, but the scales were too thick for his tiny teeth to inflict any damage. The thing didn't even feel his bite.

"Get down, Dick, get down!" ordered Paddy.

Obediently, Dick jumped down. Paddy threw lightning bolts at the head of the monster. The beast at once turned toward the wizard, mouth wide open, and threw a jet of poisonous slime at Paddy. Immediately, the young wizard responded with a jet of fire, which disappeared into the monster's open throat. With a big boom, it exploded into a thousand pieces.

"Wow! You are wonderful, man. I can't believe you are the same shy little boy I knew on Earth!" said Daryl, patting his earth buddy on the shoulder.

Paddy smiled. "Well, now I am an elf, and a wizard. That is the difference. Even on Earth, I had all this in me, but I didn't know it. Niko helped me to discover it."

The boys and Dick came over and Tony said, "We don't understand. We were just playing with Dick, throwing a piece of wood, and it became a monster."

"It was the sorcerer in action. That is why I insist on your staying nearby. You understand, now?" asked Paddy.

"I am sorry, Prince Paddy. I promise we won't go far any more," said Tony.

"Good. I am glad you have learned your lesson. Too bad it had to be the hard way," replied Paddy.

Dick, head down, sat at Tony's feet. After all, it was he who called the boys to play.

"I congratulate you, Dick, on your obedience," the elf said, looking at the dog. Dick's tail wagged slowly. He felt miserable. The boys had been scolded because of him. Even the brilliant sun above, the birds singing in the grove, and the little rabbits munching the grass couldn't lift the dog's spirit. Dick looked at them with a mournful eye.

"What's wrong, boy?" asked Zyra, kneeling beside him.

"He feels guilty," replied Daryl, knowing his dog well.

"Why Dick? You must not!" said the two young boys.

"All right, enough of self-pity, Dick. Let's eat!" said Paddy, laughing, "I am sure everybody is starving, even you, Dick?"

"Yes! Yes!" cried Daryl and the boys in unison. Dick let out a faint bark.

"Come on, Dick! You can be more enthusiastic than that!" said Tony and Zyra laughing. Dick's guilt left him. He joined the chorus and barked joyously. Sabrina danced around him with her doll in her arms. They sat in a circle.

Thanks to Paddy the most delicious breakfast appeared. Vald had a fresh bale of clover, fruits, and a large pall of water. Silence filled the air, and only the songs of the birds was heard. Dick had forgotten all his troubles. His eyes shone and licking his lips, he sat beside his master, waiting to be fed. As soon as the meal was over they left.

Leaving the beautiful valley, a bare deserted country with rough hills awaited them. They walked for hours. The boys kept their promise and stayed close to the men. Vald, deep in thought, distractedly looked at Sabrina, and noticed that she was having a hard time walking on the rocks. The kind giant gently picked her up and sat the little elf upon his shoulder.

"Thank you, Vald. I was getting very tired."

"Well! You do look like a queen on her throne," teased Tony.

"So. What's wrong with that?" she asked her brother.

"Nothing."

He giggled, elbowing Zyra in the ribs.

Sabrina ignored him. From up here she could see further than the others. What she saw worried her. "There is something moving on the side of that hill. Lots of things."

"What are they? Can you describe them for me?" asked Paddy.

"I think it is a large band of Urks."

"Urks! Not again, man," said Daryl.

"Vald, will you please hold me up," asked Paddy.

Vald lowered his hand, and the elf jumped in. The giant lifted his arm high above his head. "I see them very well. They are not Urks."

"What are they?" asked Daryl with a sigh of relief.

Chapter 39

"Nomads! A tribe that goes from village to village. Entertainment is their business, not fighting or killing."

"Good!" cried Sabrina. "We are going to see the clowns."

Tony said, "Months ago they visited our Realm. We all came down from the trees to see their show. It was nice,"

"They visited our village, too. We had a good time," said Zyra.

"I see that you are acquainted with them. What about you, Vald?" asked Paddy.

"Valdos are not much for that sort of thing," replied the giant.

"We, too, have that on Earth. It's called the circus. Remember, man? Mom took us with your sister to see them. It was fun," said Paddy.

"Oh, yes." He laughed. "Do you remember when I caught the monkey, and tied his tail with a ribbon around his neck? How he became wild." Daryl was laughing to tears at the memory of his naughty act.

"Yes, I do. I also remember how fast you ran when his master came after you with a big stick," Paddy replied with a chuckle.

"True!" Daryl laughed.

"You surely were a mean boy," said Tony.

"Yes, I was! Paddy can testify to that, but we had a good time together."

"Most of the time I was scared to death by his daring acts."

"Let's go on, and meet the Baladins," said Tony, who was excited by the idea.

Sabrina looked worried and said, "You are not going to do some bad things to them, are you, Daryl?"

"No, Sabrina, I am not a foolish boy anymore," replied Daryl, walking away still laughing.

It took them the good part of an hour to reach the band. There were about one hundred of them, with small carts pulled by ponies. They were a different race from the elves, a very handsome people, much taller, with light brown skin, black curly hair, and light green eyes. They were a peaceful people, who dwelt in the elfic realm in small tribes. This group belonged to the Wildcat Tribe. Paddy introduced himself and his friends to the chief of the band. "We are on a quest. Would you mind, friend, if we were to join you for a while?"

"Not at all," replied the chief, whose name was Gugar. "We will be honored to have you with us," he said, bowing to Paddy.

Zyra left his friends to talk with the young boys. He felt very much at ease with these simple folks. Tony and Sabrina enjoyed their friendliness, too. The children had a marvelous time. The young ones proudly showed the strangers the circus animals and the clown's carts, where they hung their colorful clothes.

When they stopped to set camp for the night they sent the children to collect wood in the desert. They left, laughing, followed by Zyra. Tony and Sabrina looked at Paddy.

"I am sorry, but you must stay here," he said to them.

"Why?" asked Gugar, "There is no danger here."

"Oh, yes, Chief. There is danger for them, unfortunately," replied Paddy.

The chief didn't answer. He looked at the young elf, asking no more questions. The children sighed. A little later, the young nomads and Zyra came back with several large bundles of wood.

"Where did they find that? There is no wood around here," said Daryl.

The chief smiled. "They are used to seeing what untrained eyes don't see," he replied.

"They certainly do! I haven't see a single piece of wood on our way coming here," said Daryl with admiration.

The chief proudly replied, "This is our way of life,"

That night the fire was burning high. The children had collected enough wood for the entire night. They wanted to entertain their guests handsomely! First they served an excellent meal, and to finish the evening the clowns put on a show for the children. They started out with simple little magic tricks, of which they were very proud. Paddy didn't reveal that he was a wizard, and didn't offer to provide anything for the evening entertainment. He did not want to embarrass anyone.

The little ponies had been well fed and were sleeping in a small corral near the carts. The night was pitch black, with no stars or moon, and this pleased the clowns. Quietly, they disappeared to get dressed. The audience sat in a half-circle in front of the big fire. For a reason unknown to the travelers, they had left the part facing the crowd completely empty, and dark.

The children were giggling with anticipation. Suddenly, from behind the fire came the sound of a violin and an accordion. To their delight, the clowns emerged from the night, dressed in their beautiful clothes, which shone in the light. Laughing and playing their musical instrument they flew over the fire, their legs beating the air. Poof! One fell into the fire producing lots of sparks. The children screamed! Magically, up he went, and down again still playing his lively music. Realizing it was a game, the children applauded, laughing.

More clowns came to jump high above the flames, stopped in midair and screamed, terrified! Their legs, like puppet's legs, kept running in the air and with their arms wrapped around their heads they hung suspended, screaming and calling for help! They finally giggled and, dancing above the fire, pushed the musician clowns out into the dark.

Dick was quite blasé about the performance and had gone to sleep beside his master a long time ago. The performance went on, and on, with new tricks, for hours. Tired from laughing, the children, too, had fallen asleep.

"Good night, Gugar, it was a marvelous show," said Paddy.

"Good night friends. If you want, it won't take us long to put up a tent for you."

"No, thank you, we will be fine. Good night," replied the elf. Quietly they covered the children with their elfic capes, then did the same for themselves, and went to sleep. Vald took Dick, still asleep, under his cape.

* * *

The next morning Paddy realized the nomads were not going the same way as his little party was, so he said goodbye and gave thanks for their hospitality. Sorry to see their guests leaving so soon, the nomads sadly said, farewell. Giggling and playing, the young nomads followed their new friends for a while. As soon as Daryl noticed that the Nomad children were too far from the group, with a cheerful smile he sent them back to the caravan. Regretfully the children left.

It had been hours since they left the band. Now, at the summit of the last rugged hill, their dry, tired eyes saw, far below, a lovely green country, with lakes and groves. What a restful sight it was, after the sandy hills. On the horizon emerged the dark line of a large forest.

"At last, trees and water, man," said Daryl.

Coming from nowhere a big black cloud covered the lovely picture. Thick, dark, fog fell upon everything in the valley.

"Where has the sun gone?" asked Tony.

Evil laughter resounded.

"Xary!" said Vald, terrified

"He knows how dangerous it will be for us to travel in that fog with all those lakes," replied Paddy.

"How are we going to go through that?" asked Daryl.

"With lots of care, man."

"We could get lost, separated from each other. Then he will get me," said the poor, trembling Vald.

"No, Vald, don't be afraid. I am going to tie us together with a magic rope."

"But, he can cut it in the fog. We won't even notice it," said Vald.

"Not the one I am going to bind us with. Don't worry."

"Are you sure?" asked Vald, still not reassured.

"We will put you between us. Paddy in the front and me following you." said Daryl cheerfully.

'Vald, you must carry the children and Dick," said Paddy.

"Of course," replied Vald.

"All right, let's get organized then," said Daryl.

"Tony and Zyra, you get on our friend's shoulders. Hang on tight, you could be knocked down by a branch. Sabrina and Dick in Vald's arms," said Paddy. "Is that fine with you, Vald?" asked the elf.

"Perfectly fine."

"Now, the rope. Please stand in the order we are going to travel."

From down below resounded Xary's terrible laughter.

"You may laugh all you want, but you won't get us, any more than the other times," mumbled Paddy.

Daryl, Vald, with the children and Dick, were in position. The wizard faced them and moved his hand, whispering something. "There, we are linked," he said.

"I don't see anything man. Where is it?" said Daryl.

"Well, try moving away from Vald."

Daryl, always skeptical, began to walk away. He was immediately pulled back as if he had a rope around his waist. "Well, are you convinced?"

"Yes, thank you, " replied Daryl, ashamed of his doubts.

"Okay, we are all set? Let's go," said Paddy.

They walked down the hill. "It will be a long way before we reach the bottom. I'm hungry. Let's stop to eat. That will show Xary we are not scared of him, and that we still have good appetites," said Daryl, laughing.

"He is probably anxiously waiting for us down there." Tony giggled.

They all sat and ate. Once the meal was over the boys stretched their legs by chasing Dick without going away from the group. Soon the time came for the children to resume their place on Vald's shoulders, and the little party left. The way down to the valley was long.

"I think we should sleep here, man. It will be safer than down in the valley in the fog," suggested Daryl.

"The voice of wisdom has spoken. You are getting wiser in your old age," Paddy replied with a chuckle.

"Thank you, your lordship." Daryl bowed, sweeping the air with his right hand.

Everybody laughed. Night had come. They were near a big rock formation and Paddy said, "This is a suitable place for us. We will be protected from any attack coming from behind."

"Perfectly good idea" replied Vald, looking around, his gentle eyes, betraying his fear.

Paddy moved his hand to smooth the ground. After a short meal they covered their faces with their hoods, and went to sleep. Dick crawled under Daryl's cape, and soon he gently snored. The night had neither stars nor moon. Only Xary's red eyes watched the travelers.

Paddy in his mind heard him saying, "You may rest. Tomorrow, I will get you. You have a busy day ahead."

He left. His evil laughter shook the valley. Dick growled, and the young wizard smiled in his sleep.

The night had been peaceful. Paddy knew that Xary was watching every move they made.

"One thing is certain. The sorcerer is waiting for us in the fog," said Paddy.

"This is so frightening, and not at all comforting to me," replied Vald.

"I know. Unfortunately, other trials are waiting for us. But we will destroy him, Vald," said the young wizard.

"I am not too fussy about going down there, either, Vald," said Daryl with a grimace.

"Let's get moving, guys."

Quietly the children and the dog went to Vald for transportation. Paddy led the way, with Vald behind. Daryl brought up the rear. The sky was gray and down below crawled the very thick fog. Half an hour later they were into it.

"Wow. It's difficult to see anything at all, man," mumbled Daryl.

"I will try to make it lighter," Paddy said as he began to move his hands. Nothing happened.

"I tell you, the sorcerer has put lots of power into this fog. I can't move it."

A terrible laughter resounded. Vald shivered.

"He is going to get us," he said.

"No, he won't, Vald. This is a very good thing that he has put so much power into the fog. He will have less for battle and tricks." Paddy laughed.

"Are you sure of that?" asked the poor, trembling Vald.

"Yes! His power is not that great, and that is why he wants your horns. Follow me. We have the rope to keep us together," said the elf.

They moved silently, carefully. The greatest danger was falling into a lake and being drowned, by Xary and his creatures.

"Yes," whispered Paddy, "that is his plot." With that certitude, the young wizard sent a spell ahead to keep them away from the water. "You don't have us yet," he mumbled.

The ground was easy to walk. It would have taken lots of power from the sorcerer to change it, and he didn't have any left to speak of. Paddy's spell was guiding their steps. Furious, Xary fussed around. Hours later, his rage got fiercer. The fog lightened up a bit. The evil one was burning so much energy in his anger that he couldn't maintain the fog.

Paddy smiled, whispering, "Good. Very good. Soon you will be powerless and will have to return to your lair."

Paddy chuckled at the thought and screamed in the same breath.

Chapter 40

A large hole engulfed them. Vald's weight pulled everybody down. The boys on his shoulders hung on to his horns. Daryl screamed his head off.

Paddy moved his hand quickly, reducing the speed and cut the magic rope holding them together. Held by the power of the young wizard, they arrived sound and safe at the bottom of the pit. Tony and Sabrina had flown down, but Zyra, who couldn't get at his cape, still hung onto Vald's horn. The giant had Dick in his arms.

"What happened, man?" asked Daryl who was badly shaken.

"Sorry, it's my fault, guys. When I put a spell to guide my steps away from waters, I should have added accidents in the ground."

"Where are we, man? Is this Xary's doing?"

"No, he is going to be furious when he notices our disappearance."

"I am surely glad of that," said Vald.

Paddy looked around. There were steps going further down. "Let's take those stairs. It can't be worse than Xary's rage,"

"Steps! My goodness. There are tunnels and steps everywhere in your realm, going to the depths of the earth! It's like a Swiss cheese," said Daryl.

"What's that?" asked the boys.

"Never mind," replied Daryl.

"We have many kingdoms of dwarves. They are industrious people, mining copper, iron, gold, silver, and many other things such as precious gems and diamonds. That is the reason, man."

The steps were small. Vald had difficulty finding a place for his large feet and took three or four steps at a time. Daryl, blind in the dark, pulled his elfic stone out.

"Why do you do that?" asked Tony, walking behind him.

"I like to see where I put my feet."

"But they are just steps, one after the other."

"Logic of children! I know that," he mumbled, offended.

They arrived at the bottom of the stairs.

"What's there, man?" asked Daryl.

"A large cave in white marble," replied Paddy.

"Wow" said Daryl, lighting the cave with his stone.

Under the gentle light the walls shone softly. Then a sweet voice said, "Welcome to our realm. Please enter."

They went through the shining wall. Beautiful lights shone on their hair, their eyes, and on their skin.

On the other side of the lights a girl and a boy waited for them. Both were handsome youngsters, dressed in white velvet, with gold bands around their heads, and gold slippers on their feet.

They smiled and said, "Please follow us."

"Where are we?" asked Paddy. There was no reply, only a smile. The hall they went through was in pink marble. Chandeliers of gold and crystal gave a gentle light. The long golden hair of the little girl swayed behind her, and the boy's black hair shone like raven's wing. A sort of reverence was about. They reached a high golden gate. The young boy touched it with a diamond he wore on his right hand. Silently, the gate opened.

"Wow! This is cool, man." Daryl's eyes were round like saucers.

Gentle harp music floated in the room. Sylphs, dressed in long gold gowns, whispered as they walked about. In the hall pink velvet chairs and sofas waited for anyone to sit, rest, or meditate. At the center of the lovely room was a big round table of white marble, with a beautiful gold vase full of flowers. High amber pedestals had censers of gold burning perfume at the corners of the room. A crystal chandelier gave peaceful light in the quiet room.

Without a word, they went to the right. The boy stopped in front of an ivory door. The young girl touched it, and it quietly opened.

A deep voice said, "Welcome to the Realm of Serenity. I am Lord

Serenio."

On a throne of gold sat a man, with hair and beard white as snow, kindly and large blue eyes.

"Salutations, Lord Serenio. I am Prince Patrick, elf from the Promised Valley, traveling on a quest with my friends."

"Welcome, and greetings to all of you. You have entered the Realm of Serenity."

All bowed their heads and Dick wagged his tail politely. Lord Serenio rang a small crystal bell. The young boy came. "Light, my younger son, will be your guide and will help you in your desires."

The young boy bowed his head.

"Go, be happy with us." Lord Serenio vanished in a thousand lights.

"Wow! How did he do that?" asked Daryl.

The young boy replied proudly, "My father is a Lord of Lights."

"Of course, I should know," said Daryl, bowing, making fun of the boy.

Surprised, Tony asked, "Why do you act like that?"

"For nothing, it's just me. Probably all these fantastic things happening in this realm are getting to me."

"Why?"

"Because what's normal for you is not for me. I guess I will get used to it with time. On Earth, we don't have all this magic. That's all."

Light gently touched the door with his ring. Silently, it opened. They crossed the lovely pink hall. Many fair people bowed as they passed.

"Where are we going?" asked Daryl.

"To meet my mother.

"Your mother! Why?" asked Daryl, who was becoming alarmed, afraid that strange things might happen again.

"When we receive visitors, they all meet my mother," replied the boy, smiling.

"Do you have many strangers coming?" asked Daryl.

"Not often. The last visit was not too long ago."

199

"How long ago?" Daryl wanted to get to the bottom of the story. How come they have visitors, in a place where you have to fall into a hole in the ground to get there.

"About two hundred years."

"What! Two hundred years! And you call that not long ago!"

"It's not," smiled Light. "I am only one thousand years old."

"One thous…!" Daryl choked.

Tony laughed. "So what? He is very young for our realm."

"How old are you, then?"

"Well, just a little younger, seven hundred years. Sabrina is only five hundred years."

Tony and Zyra giggled, watching Daryl's face. The human was quiet for the rest of the walk.

Suddenly, Dick ran to a beautiful brown door, framed by shining red stone. The dog barked, and went through it.

Light screamed, "Don't go there! You will die! It's the Pass of Darkness!'

No one listened to the screaming boy. Daryl ran after Dick and everybody followed him. The door quietly closed behind them.

"Where are we? It's so dark! Even with my night vision I can't see well," said Tony.

"Neither can I," replied Paddy.

Daryl brought out his elfic stone. The little blue light in this dreadful place was very, very dim. They never had experienced such darkness.

"Dick, Dick, where are you?" called Daryl. A small whimper answered.

"Here he is," said Vald.

Dick, utterly terrified, was curled up in the middle of whatever it was they where in.

"There, there, boy," said Vald, picking him up.

With his hair standing up like a porcupine, poor Dick was trembling like a leaf in a high wind. Paddy looked around to see what was scaring the dog so much. Nothing was visible. When they entered the void they were in, the door behind them had disappeared.

200

They couldn't return. Paddy tried many wizard spells. Nothing worked.

Suddenly, growling and hissing surrounded them. Phosphorescent eyes shone in the deep darkness, slobbering jaws with long fangs snapped at them.

"Wow! This is what Dick smelled, much before we saw those horrible things," said Daryl, as he too avoided the fangs.

"How are we going to escape?" asked Vald, who turned round and round to avoid the monster's jaws. His horns were scratching the roof with a shrilling, whistling, grating sound.

Then, sparks, thunder, and a rustling wind shook the void. The monsters howled in terror. The roof flew in pieces into the air. A large hole appeared and sucked the screaming friends up into the funnel of a tornado!

Chapter 41

Stars in a beautiful sky shone around them.

"We are outside," cried Sabrina, hanging onto Vald.

"What happened?" asked Tony.

"I think it has something to do with Vald's horns," replied Paddy.

"How come?" asked Zyra.

Paddy said, "When Vald spun around, his magic horns scratched the roof, and they creating a very strong spell which pulled us out of that horrible void."

"Now, where are we going, man?" asked Daryl, who was feeling terrified at being in the twisting funnel.

"We will see," replied the elf.

"This is fun!" said Tony, laughing. "I love it!"

"I don't" replied Sabrina, holding onto Vald's fur and her doll.

"I would have been very surprised if you did," replied her brother.

Vald, with Dick in his arms, was not buffeted in the funnel. Daryl had a terrible time and could only feel as if he was on a boat in rough water. He was not an elf, to enjoy the ride. They stayed inside the tornado for several hours. Poor Daryl, sick and exhausted, thought his last hour had come. The golden sun appeared on the horizon and far below was a nice valley.

"If only we were landing there," whined Daryl.

The tornado was still rustling into the sky. "Are we going to stay here forever?" asked Daryl in despair.

"I don't know, man," replied Paddy.

"Can't you do anything?" asked Daryl, pale as a ghost.

"I tried. I tried! Nothing works! I am going to put a spell on you to stop your motion sickness," said Paddy.

"Oh, thank you," said Daryl in a faint voice.

"Perhaps Vald should help. They are his horns, and his spell," said Zyra.

"Good thinking, boy. All right, Vald, do something," said the human who was now feeling better, thanks to Paddy's spell.

Surprised, the giant looked at him. "What do you want me to do, Daryl?" he asked.

"I don't know! They are your horns, not mine. Hurry!" replied Daryl. "I have enough of being tossed in the air. I am not a bird, you know!"

Vald scratched his head. "I really don't know what to do, Daryl. Oh, I wish we were in the valley below resting under a nice tree." he sighed. A second later they were on the ground under a big tree.

"You did it! You did it, Vald," sang Sabrina, dancing on the grass around him.

Daryl, flat on his back, sighed. "Is our quest over, Paddy?"

"No, man. We will rest for a while at my father's palace. Xary is still well and alive, and remember, and we must destroy him. Now, Vald, about that Power of yours. You have to learn how to use it."

"I know. I will need help."

"You will have it. I will have my uncle Niko guide you," replied Paddy.

For the next few hours they enjoyed peace and friendship under the big tree, talking about the quest, and what they had learned through their adventures.

"Daryl, my dearest Earthly chum, you have learned to share and be charitable. Tony, young prince, you know now how to be a leader. Zyra, you have all the qualities of a courageous squire, and you, little Sabrina, have shown great courage. Now, we are ready to go home. I will ask our friend, Vald, to exercise his great power by wishing us to the Realm of the Promised Valley."

"It will be an honor and a pleasure for me," replied the gentle giant. "You must come closer. Please hold onto me."

Vald once more leaned down and took Dick into his arms, saying, "We don't want to leave you behind, little friend."

Dick whimpered, and barked joyously.

Vald, in a thunderous voice, said, "All right. I wish to be in the Realm of the Promised Valley."

In the space of seconds they were in the beautiful valley. It was full of flowers and orchards, with elves singing while working.

Paddy said, joyously, "MY REALM!"

"How marvelous. I don't want to ever live in a realm where there is no magic," said Daryl, laughing.

"This is the elves' realm. It is magic, man. We all have magic in ourselves," replied Paddy.

"I want to stay here forever, man." Anxiously he asked, "Would it be possible?"

"Of course, if it's what you want, man." Paddy laughed, giving a big slap on Daryl's back."

"But, Daryl will have to become an elf like us. Otherwise he will grow old very fast, and die," said Tony.

"I want to be an elf. I don't want to be a mortal!"

"All right, all right! Later on, we will see with the King," replied Paddy.

"The King? Oh man, I forgot. It is so strange to think that you are a real prince. During the quest we were companions, old friends from the Earth Realm. Now, you are a prince, and so is Tony, and little Sabrina is a princess." Daryl sighed, and looked sadly at Paddy.

"Why that big sigh, man?"

"Once more we are going to be separated, this time by your rank," replied Daryl.

"No, we won't! I am going to take you as my squire, just like Tony has taken Zyra. You have proved your courage during the quest. You will be made a knight."

"Really? A knight!" cried Daryl.

"Yes, man, and a very good one."

"I remember, a long time ago, one day when we were kids in the Earth Realm, you passed me running, screaming, I have the heart of a knight! I have the heart of a knight. I thought you were crazy. Now I feel like doing the same," said Daryl with a chuckle.

"I remember that! My uncle Niko had just told me that. I was so happy. For a chicken heart like mine, it was a great compliment."

It was so good to have no fear of evil around. Dick barked at all the dogs he met on his way. He played with them, bouncing happily, and returning to his master.

At last the children were children again, playing and screaming joyously with the young elves along the road.

"Here it is! My HOME, man," said Paddy proudly to Daryl.

"Wow! I can't believe that I, Daryl, will actually enter a palace to meet a king and a real queen."

"And a queen that you actually know, boy. Remember, she was on Earth with me at the cottage when we were children."

"Yes. Oh! That's terrible. She will remember all the bad things I did."

"I guess so," Paddy replied with a chuckle.

In the sunshine, the trumps blared, announcing the return of Prince Patrick. The elves dropped what they were doing, arriving running from everywhere. The young prince was loved by all.

King Ariol and Queen Tara were waiting at the top of the palace's stairs. Paddy arrived, bouncing, and bowed to his royal parents (this was the protocol) then fondly kissed them.

"Father, I have great news. Through our efforts, Xary's power has been neutralized for a while."

The crowd cheered.

He added, "I would like you to meet our friend, Vald, of the Valdos tribe."

"I know the Valdos. Quiet and strong people," replied the King.

"And now, Father, Mother, may I present my old friend Daryl from the Earth Realm."

"Daryl!" cried the Queen, "Daryl, I remember you, young man. I am very glad you came to our realm. Welcome." The Queen smiled. "I am sure you and Paddy will have plenty to talk about."

Daryl bowed. The young human, certain that the Queen remembered all his mischief, turned red. Paddy saw Daryl's embarrassment and immediately came to his rescue, saying, "Father,

Mother, I present Prince Tony and his sister Princess Sabrina from the Realm of the Flying Elves. He is a very courageous young elf. Because of his help we were able to pursue our quest. Later, you will learn why these young people are with us."

Zyra shyly hid himself behind Vald.

The King smiled. "Now, who is this young elf behind Vald?" he asked.

"I was coming to him, Father. He is a courageous member of our party. His name is Zyra, and he comes from the Elves of the Shining Waters, and he is Prince Tony's squire."

Dick sat in front of the royal couple and boldly barked.

King Ariol laughed. "Well, I see that you are introducing yourself. Welcome, Dick, little friend. I am certain you have been of great value to the quest."

The dog barked twice, wagged his tail, and went to sit by his master's side.

"Here is someone without complication, just like Tiger. They will be very good friends, I am sure," said the Queen, smiling.

"You are right, Father. Dick has been of great value to us and has saved our lives several times."

When the royal couple turned around to enter the palace, the elves cheered. Happily, they continued singing, dancing, and sharing the good news with those who arrived late.

Paddy, with his friends, followed the King and his court inside. The chamberlain came to escort the guests to their rooms.

The young elf said to his friends, "I will see you later. Daryl, you come with me. You are now my squire, therefore you sleep in a room beside mine."

Daryl sighed. "Good. I was so scared to be lost in this great house of yours, prince! If you had told me that, years ago on Earth, for sure I would have thought you were completely crazy." Daryl chuckled at the thought.

' Talking and laughing, they went through splendid halls of pink marble, with crystal chandeliers. They climbed a large staircase and arrived in a green marble hall with gold chandeliers. Paddy opened a massive oak door.

"There, man. This is my room."

Daryl's mouth stayed opened. Never in his born life had he seen anything like this. The sun freely entered through large bow windows. The room was a sort of study-library-living room with dark green velvet curtains and lighter green leather chairs. On the floor was a thick burgundy rug. Precious furniture shone softly around the room. Books, colorfully bound in leather, were on shelves lining the walls. Near to it was Paddy's bedroom and bathroom.

"Wow!"

"Come," he said to Daryl.

Paddy opened a door in his study leading to a room, a little bit smaller, with large windows, almost the replica of Paddy's room, only with different colors. Books on shelves were around the walls. Daryl looked at them with a funny face. Paddy laughed. "I know, man, books have never been among your best friends. Your bedroom is next door. You see, you are beside me."

"My room! Are you joking, man?'

"No, it's yours. You will find all you need. The tailor will come to take your measurements for your clothes. You are my squire and must be dressed accordingly."

"Wow! Don't know what to say, man."

"Fine. Suits me. We'll see you later. I am going to arrange with the King for you to become an elf, if that's still your wish?"

"You bet!"

Paddy left to change and clean up. Daryl, uncertain about what to do, looked around, then slowly moved to the desk, sat in the big chair, and gently ran his hand on the top. Then he jumped up and went to his bedroom and to the bathroom. "I am going to take a shower."

Satisfied with his decision, whistling for joy, he scrubbed thoroughly, got dressed, and walked to the balcony where he sat until dark. Paddy found him there. Daryl said, "This is the most beautiful night since I left Earth."

Chapter 42

"I am sorry, you surely haven't had much rest since you came to our realm."

"I loved the quest. It was great. I am starved, man. When are we going to eat?"

Paddy laughed. "Just a minute. First things first, Okay? I have talked to the King, and the Wizard Niko, my uncle, about you becoming an elf. They don't object. Tomorrow they will prepare the ceremony."

"Ceremony!" cried Daryl, forgetting about his claim of hunger. "I thought they just gave you a piece of paper."

"No, man. You have to change, to become like us. Otherwise you will age and die."

"Oh, I see." The word ceremony had really scared him.

"Let's go to eat," said Paddy to change his thoughts.

"Yes. I am starved."

"My parents won't be dining with us. They have a reception to attend."

"Fine with me, man. I was petrified at the idea of eating at a royal table. The very thought of it scared me so much that I was losing my appetite," he said nervously.

* * *

The next morning Daryl woke up in his splendid bedroom. First, he looked around not very sure of where he was. He sat up, rubbed his head, and painfully started to assort the past and present events in his mind. Then he felt much better. Later on the tailor came to spend an hour with him, taking his measurements.

After the tailor left, Daryl looked outside. Elfic gardeners were busy cutting flowers for the palace. It was so lovely and peaceful. Paddy knocked at the door and joyously entered.

"The tailor came to take my measurements. It was like the undertaker taking them for my box. I didn't like that too much." He made a face.

Paddy laughed. "Come on, man. I am sure it was cool." Daryl looked at his friend, not certain where the fun was. "The preparation for your ceremony is underway. This afternoon you will be an elf."

"Does it hurt?" asked Daryl fearfully.

"No, silly. It is beautiful. You'll see."

"Do I have to do something?"

"No."

"Sounds safe enough."

"It is. Come to eat. The tailor promised to have one of your suits done for this afternoon."

The two boys left the palace. Paddy wanted to introduce Daryl to the academy. After a good time with Paddy's young friends, Daryl returned to his rooms. The tailor had kept his word. On the bed was a splendid pair of dark purple velvet pants with a long white satin tunic and a gold belt. To finish the outfit there was a pair of soft white leather boots.

"Wow! I will look like a prince!"

Paddy rapped at Daryl's door, and quietly entered. "Wow! Look at you! You are an elf already!"

"I can't believe what I see! I was an old man! Now I am a fifteen-year- old boy dressed like a prince," replied Daryl.

"Yes, I know, man. That's why I went to earth to get you."

"Thank you, Paddy. My useless life was ending. You filled it with purpose. With you I did something good. I want to continue to help."

"You will soon. The quest is not over yet. Let's go now to the palace garden where the ceremony has been prepared for you."

"Oh, gosh! I am so nervous!"

"Don't be, man! It's beautiful. You will love it!"

"But I am not used to being the center of attention. It's scary.'"

Paddy smiled, remembering years ago when he and his mom had

gone through it, and how scared he had been, too.

Hundreds of elves were gathered in the alleys of the garden. At the edge of a small meadow a platform had been erected for the royal family and court.

Daryl backed up. "You think I will go there, alone, in front of all those people? No way, man!"

"Yes. But you won't be alone, Daryl. I will be with you. Dick will be there carried by Vald. You need two witnesses. Vald asked to be the second, and I, the first. We will be with you all the way."

Daryl sighed. With his companions of the quest at his side, he could face anything. "I feel better. Let's go then. I am glad to have both of you with me." Daryl beamed.

Paddy gave him a slap on his shoulder. "Good. Come now."

Vald arrived with Dick in his arms. The three friends looked each other square in the eyes and walked to where the royal couple sat with the court. The three bowed their head to them and took their place in the center of a large ring of flowers held by young Elfic boys. Paddy and Vald stood on each side of Daryl. Then, from the right, a string of young girls arrived, singing, playing on small Irish harps. They walked slowly behind the boys to take their place, forming another circle.

On a platform high above where the King and Queen were sitting, stood Niko the great wizard, the King's brother, Paddy's uncle who brought him to the elves' realm. The wizard raised his arms up in front of him. Immediately Vald gave Dick to Daryl. Dick understood the moment was extremely important for his master and him. So, very quietly, he sat at Daryl's feet. If Vald had kept the dog in his arms that would have prevented Dick from becoming an elfic dog. Vald was already a member of the realm.

The girls hummed very sweetly. The wizard uttered powerful words that Daryl didn't understand. Out of the wizard's hands flashed multicolor sparkling lights, which gently fell in thousands of stars onto the little group. Then a misty veil covered them. Only the music of harps was heard. The mist disappeared, and a cheerful song started. The boys danced, clapping their hands while the girls cast flowers onto the friends.

Paddy hugged his friend. "There, you are an elf, man."

Vald shook his hand said, "I am glad you are going to stay with us, Daryl."

"So am I. So am I. Is that all?"

"Yes. What did you expect, man? How do you feel?"

"Light, very light! Really, I am an elf? Yes. I am. My ears are pointed, like yours, and now I can hear the animals on the farms very far away. Wonderful! Wonderful," Daryl kept repeating.

"Yes, you are, and so is Dick."

Dick barked. In answer to his barking, two balls of fur rushed into the circle.

"I see, Dick, you are receiving the congratulations from your friends, Tiger and Mitsou," said Paddy, laughing.

The King and Queen welcomed the new elf to their realm. The crowd cheered and immediately the festivities started. There were dances, songs, and food, Daryl's favorite thing. To Daryl's delight they danced, and ate, for weeks. Elves are joyous people. When they are merry, they are merry! But they never neglect their duties. At night, they returned home and as soon as the chores were finished, they joyously came back to the feast and kept this up until harvest time! Daryl ate, and ate! So did Dick with his new friends Tiger and Mitsou.

When everything was over, the new elf started his training as a squire. New adventures were waiting ahead, and this time Daryl wanted to be ready to meet the challenges, and serve Prince Paddy well.

Vald, with the teaching and help of Niko the Great Wizard, learned how to use his power, and returned to the Valdos Tribe as their wizard.

King Urzy and Queen Kyra, Tony and Sabrina's parents, arrived. The happy youngsters had so much to tell about the quest. Especially Tony! How he and Zyra had endured many hardships to retrieve the ring from the old gremlin's finger.

The King smiled, proud of his son's courage. "One day you will be a good king, my son," he said to Tony.

Zyra's parents also arrived. Later, the family departed with the King and his escort for the Realm of the Flying Elves.

They announced proudly, "Our son will enter the academy to become young Prince Tony's squire."

Stoy, Niko's son, was glad to have his cousin Paddy back. He promised himself with great fervor that from now on he would never let Paddy or Daryl out of sight. "Someday they will leave to finish the quest. This time, I will go."

The trio became inseparable, as were the three dogs, Tiger, Mitsou and Dick.

At night, the elves would sit around the fire with their excited children, recounting the great quest. The quest when Prince Paddy, his mortal friend Daryl, and Vald the giant fought the evil Sorcerer Xary. How young Prince Tony restored to Paddy his power lost in a fight with the goblins, by taking the magic ring from the old gremlin's finger, making it possible for the teen adventurers to continue their quest. The beautiful green eyes of the young elves would shine, as they would dream, in the secret of their hearts, of fabulous quests, of going one day to fight a wicked sorcerer.

Au Revoir et a Bientot
With *Paddy and Daryl*
At The Portal of Evil

Printed in the United States
36341LVS00002B/10-57

9 781413 777802